GIFT OF

John Warren Stewig

Carthage

Margaret's Moves

by Berniece Rabe

illustrated by Julie Downing

E. P. DUTTON   NEW YORK

Library of Congress Cataloging in Publication Data

Rabe, Berniece.
    Margaret's moves.
    Summary: Nine-year-old Margaret, confined to a wheelchair
by spina bifida, longs for a new, lightweight sports-model
chair so that she can speed around as fast as the athletic
brother with whom she has an ongoing rivalry.
    [1. Spina bifida—Fiction. 2. Physically handicapped
—Fiction. 3. Brothers and sisters—Fiction]
I. Downing, Julie, ill. II. Title.
PZ7.R105Mar 1986 [Fic] 86-11592
ISBN 0-525-44271-5

Published in the United States by E. P. Dutton,
2 Park Avenue, New York, N.Y. 10016

Published simultaneously in Canada by
Fitzhenry & Whiteside Limited, Toronto

Editor: Julie Amper   Designer: Annie Alleman

Printed in the U.S.A.   W   First Edition
10 9 8 7 6 5 4 3 2 1

to Justin Rabe

Contents

An Eye on the Sky

Margaret had been looking at the sky all morning. The clouds were thin and white and raced with her as she wheeled her chair around the circle at the end of Madras Court. Her neck was getting tired from looking up, but she didn't dare rest, even for a minute. Yesterday she'd kept watch all day except for going inside for lunch. Wouldn't you know it, one of the balloons had landed in the park, just one street over, during lunch. One of the Bernstein twins had found it. She had won a neat Flippo game.

This morning the last hundred balloons had been released from the Spring Hill Mall, and the grand prize had to be in one of them because no one had reported having won it yet. Margaret had been listening to the radio, reading the newspaper ads and the mailbox fliers for two weeks, and knew all about the mall's grand opening. She also knew exactly what she would get if she won the grand prize, a $250 gift certificate. She'd get a canopy bed like the Bernstein twins had! This was a secret wish that only her best friend, Michelle, knew about. Margaret had been saving her pennies and nickels in a secret place —a pencil box shaped like a big pencil—and only she knew there were no pencils inside.

"Rusty!" Margaret called to her brother who was messing around with Daddy's old torn-apart sports car in the garage. "Come watch with me."

"I can't," Rusty called back. "Why don't you go to the park to watch? That's where the balloons will land anyway. Michelle and the Bernstein twins can watch with you."

"Forget it, Rusty. I wouldn't stand a chance there, and you know it. Twenty houses are around that park, and all have kids except for Mr. Simmons, of course. Say, what if Mr. Simmons caught the balloon?"

"He couldn't. He's too old."

"He could, too, Rusty, if the balloon fell near his park bench. Nothing's impossible! But I know the balloon won't fall in the park today. It wouldn't fall in the same place twice."

"I thought you just said nothing was impossible?" Rusty was never too busy to argue.

"Come on! Help me watch, Rusty!"

"You can sit out there all day if you want, Margaret, but I think it's dumb."

That's precisely what Margaret planned to do. Today she wouldn't even go in to eat lunch. Some of those balloons had lots of gas and could stay up for hours. Yesterday the balloon had landed in the middle of the park right in front of the Bernsteins' house. It had traveled only a quarter of a mile. Maybe today's balloon would have just a little more gas in it and would come on over to Madras Court. It was not dumb to keep watching.

All the kids had been standing around yesterday, but then most of them had given up long before noon. This morning they had given up after thirty minutes, saying if none had come by then, they never would. But hadn't Rosalee Bernstein gotten her balloon during lunchtime? And even if none had fallen the rest of the afternoon, this was indeed a new day with new hope. It didn't have to be just like yesterday.

The clouds were like long gauze ribbons now, and there were lots of them, layer on layer . . . could that dot be? It was! An orange balloon was drifting right along with the lowest clouds, and it was coming closer and closer. It was not going to land on the next street over in the park, but right on Madras Court! She was sure of it. It was because she had hoped and prayed for it. Sometimes her hoping didn't help at all, but then other times it really worked perfectly. Margaret's heart was thunder. Her hands gripped her wheelchair arms. This was going to be one of those perfect times! The low white clouds were a bed of cotton carrying the balloon closer . . . and closer! It was going to land in the middle of the block.

Quickly, Margaret looked in all directions, calculating her chances of being the first one to it. Her mind would be her speed, since her wheelchair wasn't fast enough. This wouldn't be like the time when candy was thrown out during the parade, and the other kids beat her to it, or like when her very own best friend, Michelle, got the last cherry Popsicle from the Good Humor cart.

There were no kids on the street, except for three boys way at the other end of the block playing catch. But Margaret couldn't bank on their not noticing. If they did see it, and it was sort of hanging there now ready to land, they'd beat her to it easy.

"Rusty!" Margaret called softly. "Come get the balloon for me. I see it. It's almost landed."

Rusty could be out in a flash and beat any boy on the block to the balloon. He had been practicing running fast for eight years. He wore Nikes and thought they gave his feet wings. But why wasn't he coming now? She started moving slowly towards the balloon herself.

"Rusty!" Margaret yelled again. She was afraid to yell too loud. "Rusty, please!" Then more loudly

she yelled, "Rusty, the mall balloon's landed! Hurry! Get it for me. Quick, I'm not kidding! There! Over at the end of the vacant lot!"

At last, Rusty must have heard, because he skitted out the garage still holding something in his hand. Then he saw the balloon and *zoom!* His red head streaked by Margaret. She followed him as fast as her arms could make her wheelchair go. One day she would invent a wheelchair that would go 100 miles an hour. Uh-oh! The other boys had spotted the balloon, too, and were running for it. But it was no contest. Rusty was on top of it and had it popped before even one of them came sliding in.

"What did you get?" "Did you get the grand prize?" "What does the coupon say?" "Well, read it!" Everyone was yelling.

Margaret yelled, too. "I'll read it. I spotted it. Let me have the coupon, Rusty!" She fought her way into the midst of the clawing boys.

Rusty read, "A baseball glove. Aw, I only get a baseball glove." Any other time, Rusty would have been happy to get a baseball glove, but now everyone just moaned because it was not the grand prize.

Margaret grabbed the card and stared at it. So, her hopes hadn't gotten her the canopy bed, after all.

Rusty snatched the card back from her and said, "Anyway, this is mine. You don't play baseball, Margaret."

That was true. She didn't play baseball on the

vacant lot with Rusty and his friends. Back when she and Rusty had been a team of two, she *had* played catch with him. No more. Now, she played catch with her two-year-old brother, Tad. Tad thought she was the world's greatest catcher and pitcher, which was a much better opinion than Rusty had of her anymore.

"At least, it's half mine, Rusty. You'd never have spotted it. You were inside the garage. So, fair's fair. Tad's getting wilder and harder with his pitching, and I could use a glove. It'd make my hand reach farther. It's half mine!"

"No way, Margaret. I'm not going to split it down the center. I'm going to ride my bike over to the mall right now and get my glove."

"Ha! The mall's not open yet. Besides, during grand opening Mother wouldn't let you go alone, and you know it. We'll both go later with her. Just wait until I talk with her about it."

Rusty put the little card into his pocket and said to the boys, "What're we waiting for? Let's play ball!"

Without another word to her, they all just ran away. Margaret hated it when arguments were ended by someone walking—or worse, running— away.

"Just you wait, Rusty Sadler," she yelled after him. "I'm going to get half of this prize. You talk to me, Rusty! I could get real mad at you for this!"

Rusty didn't even look back.

Margaret decided right then and there that she was through with Rusty. He used to be nice, working *with* her instead of against her. She thought about how he used to supply the legwork, climbing up to get a cereal box from the cupboard while she figured out how to get the box open. Then they would dig out the prize and share. But Rusty didn't want to be a team now that they were older. So, she was emphatically through with him!

She didn't go in for lunch. She was so mad she didn't feel like eating. Anyway, maybe there would be a second balloon.

Michelle came running up to Margaret. She was breathless from running the three blocks to Madras Court. Her yellow curls were tight and moist from sweat. "Did you get the balloon? Who did get it? Was it the grand prize? I couldn't get to it fast enough."

"Me either." Margaret sighed and pointed towards the remains of the busted balloon. She told Michelle the whole awful story and ended by saying, "I'm skipping lunch so I can keep watch. You want to skip lunch with me, Michelle?"

"Sure. Then I'll go get us some ice cream when we're hungry. Mr. Wilet's got big round ice-cream bars on a stick at his store now. I can get you one in any colored flavor you want."

"Cherry?"

"Yum-yum. Lots of cherry."

So they sat there, Margaret in her chair and Michelle on the sidewalk curb, keeping their eyes on the sky. After a while, Michelle's mother came and picked her up to go across Portland on business and wouldn't even wait for Michelle to stop at Mr. Wilet's store first. And at three o'clock, Margaret's mother insisted that Margaret come in and eat some macaroni and cheese. Margaret started to protest, but Mother wouldn't allow her.

"The balloons have all landed for today. I know. No argument, please, Margaret. Rusty has already told me about the baseball glove. It would be very nice for you to let Rusty have this prize, dear. He's the one who'd use it daily."

"Give it to a selfish . . . !"

"Margaret, I'm sure Rusty wasn't even thinking of being selfish. Don't make a fuss about it. And please, Margaret, don't go bothering your father with this. He's about due for another trip, and he's got a lot of last-minute things on his mind."

"But Mother, I'm the one who spotted the balloon. If I hadn't, then Rusty couldn't . . ."

"That was nice of you, dear. Certainly Rusty appreciates that you told him. I'll have Daddy take Rusty along to the mall as soon as he gets home with the car. One of his errands is there. Would you mind keeping an eye on Tad while I mend that spot on your daddy's suit coat? Wish he could have managed a new one before this important trip but . . . Say, while I'm at it, I'll sew that rip in your chair cushion. I just never seem to think of it when you're not on it or when I'm not right in the middle of another job."

Margaret knew Mother worked hard to stay within their budget. They were not poor, but lots of money still went out of Daddy's paycheck each month for operations that she had had long ago because she was born with spina bifida. The last vertebrae of her spine had not formed right, and she was born paralyzed from the waist down. By the time she was two, she knew she'd never run or walk, but it didn't mean she couldn't wear some neat-looking shoes. Daddy, being an engineer for Nike, got his kids' shoes for free. Tad and Rusty wore theirs for running. Margaret wore hers because they had real class. She appreciated things with class, like that canopy bed she wanted and couldn't get because of that darn tight budget.

One of those expensive operations had been to put a shunt, a plastic tube, from her head down into her stomach so it could drain away any surplus spinal fluid. Another operation was on her spine so it would grow straight and she could sit tall and be beautiful. Both those and other minor operations had been very successful. Daddy had said, "It was worth every penny. Look how beautiful you are! Especially when you're not mad."

Well, she didn't feel beautiful now. She was still plenty mad at Rusty. But she guessed she would help Mother with Tad. At least Tad appreciated her. She went inside, got out of her wheelchair, and sat on the floor to balance a few blocks for Tad to smash down. He loved that. She guessed she really did have a talent for balancing things. One of these days, maybe she'd do some great balancing feat again like she had for the school carnival when she was in first grade.

And one of these days, she would buy the beautiful canopy bed. She'd do it without any help from Rusty, and oh-h-h-h, would he be jealous! Oh, indeed! Next time, eyes to the sky! She'd get the grand prize.

A New House Rule?

The next morning, Margaret got up when she heard Daddy's shower. Later, he peeked in her door and gave her the sign that meant a special breakfast for Mother. So Margaret got changed, finished in the bathroom, and completely dressed herself while Rusty slept on. Mother always said Rusty slept hard because he played hard. Actually he had just stayed up too late listening to everyone go on and on about his wonderful home run in baseball and the fly ball he'd caught with his new glove.

Margaret was glad to be in the kitchen alone with Daddy. While he mixed the pancake batter, Margaret put out five complete settings of silverware. "Why do I have to put spoons on the table?" she asked. "No one needs a spoon for pancakes, not even Tad."

"You know your mother's house rule on how to set a proper table. She has an eye for artistic balance, Margaret. I think you're a lot like her. You have a keen eye for balancing things."

Margaret decided to make Mother's napkin look like a flower blooming. She liked being compared to Mother.

"Well, maybe I am a good balancer," she admitted. "But I wish I were just like Rusty. I'm a year older. He has no right to be faster than me!"

"So that's what's really bothering you? You want to be equal to Rusty. Well, say, kiddo, I'm twenty-seven years older than Rusty, and he's faster than me. You don't see me losing sleep over that, do you?"

Margaret looked at Daddy and smiled. "I'm not sure. You got up before him, didn't you?" She and Daddy often had arguments which sort of became a contest to see who could outthink the other. The winner always finished with what Margaret said now. "Your argument won't hold."

Daddy laughed. "I didn't get up worrying about Rusty. In fact, I wasn't thinking of Rusty at all. I was thinking of beautiful Margaret and the beautiful table she would set, and of those light and fluffy pancakes I would make, and of how pleased your mother will be."

"Ah, Daddy, that's not fair. How can I argue when you try to flatter me? At least you and I make a good team, don't we?"

"Compared to whom?" Daddy was teasing.

Margaret wanted to say, "Compared to Rusty," but she didn't want to invite one of Daddy's lectures. Daddy was big on Margaret's being happy with herself and never being jealous. So she answered, "No one."

She heard Tad's chatter in the other room and figured she'd better get the rest of the table set fast. When Daddy was to leave on a business trip, he made breakfast as his gift-bonus to Mother for her having to manage things alone while he was gone. He liked to have this treat for her go smoothly.

Margaret made Daddy's napkin look like a pointed hat, put it on his plate, then quickly laid out Tad's bib. "Daddy, did you or Mother make the house rule that you were to make only *short* business trips if she agreed to have Tad?"

"That was no rule. That was a bargain, and we're thrilled to have Tad even if he does make a bit more work for your mother. It makes me feel good knowing you're here to give her a hand when I'm away."

Margaret accepted the compliment. Mother did have lots of jobs, such as vegetable and flower gardening, keeping the house and everyone in it clean, and stopping fights and tending anyone who got sick. Margaret tried to help with all these, but Rusty was no help at all.

Margaret asked, "When I was born, did you think I was a bargain?" She began taking down five plates from the shelf. Each was a different bright color.

"Super bargain! 'A girl!' I cried. I've always been partial to black-haired girls, ever since I met your mother."

Daddy was hamming it up for her enjoyment. So she decided to put on a show for him, too. First, she rested the plates on her lap, then she took out five matching mugs and balanced them high and perfect atop the plates. Next she balanced the entire lot in one hand and started a very slow, steady move towards the table. "And Rusty—was he a bargain, too?" she asked. She looked up just then to see Rusty standing in the kitchen doorway, watching her. It took all the steadiness she could muster to move on along in front of him. But she did it without a jiggle, jangle, or jostle.

Daddy said, "Oh, Rusty, he was the worst bargain one could ever imagine. Why he . . ." Daddy was teasing. He winked at Rusty.

Rusty just looked at Daddy and yawned and then asked, "We having pancakes? I'm starved."

Margaret said, "You know we're having pancakes. Why do you think I got out the plates-of-many-colors?" She decided she'd not put the plates and mugs on the table until Rusty noticed her superb balancing accomplishment.

Rusty said nothing. So next, Margaret moved just

a little closer to Daddy so that he could notice and compliment her if Rusty wouldn't.

Daddy did speak, and loud enough for Mother to hear him. "Come and get them while they're hot!" He flipped a pancake high in the air and caught it in the pan. Margaret loved Daddy's happy way with life. She would go ahead and set the table in an equally happy manner, even if Rusty was deliberately not noticing her talent. She would still be cheerful for Mother and Daddy's sake if Rusty never ever said one nice word.

She gave her wheel a jerk to send herself charging merrily ahead and said, "Out of my way, Rusty! I got to set the table fa-a-a-a-ast." The dishes sailed off her hand. *Slam! Bang! Crash!* They lay all over the table and floor. Faster did not mix with balancing. One plate had hit Mother's special little strawberry-shaped jar that Daddy had gotten for her on one of his trips. The lid lay broken in three pieces on the floor. Margaret bent over to pick it up, even though she knew she couldn't reach it. Anyway, it was too late to save it. The jar itself, still on the table, was cracked badly, and strawberry juice was oozing out the side.

Margaret wanted to die. Oh, how she wished this minute that she could run away and not have to see Mother's unhappy face. But she stayed. Responsible people stay and see things through to the end. She bent low to pick up the mugs quickly, grabbing for their upturned handles. She still missed. It was

Rusty who had to help her. And it was Rusty who picked up the broken pieces of the lid and threw them into the wastebasket.

He said, "You're lucky the dishes are plastic. You're really lucky none of them cracked. Why don't you carry things the right way, Margaret? I hope they make a house rule, no more balancing! Why do you have to show off?"

"Why do you have to claim all of a baseball glove that's half mine?" Margaret whispered so that Daddy could not hear.

Daddy calmly poured the strawberries from the cracked jar into his big glass measuring cup. "Don't worry about it, okay? Both of you get a smile on now before Mother comes in. Everyone has an accident once in a while." Then, Daddy dashed back to the stove to grab a smoking pan from the burner and dumped the pancake into the garbage disposal.

Obediently, Margaret tried to smile. She was glad Daddy hadn't lectured. He was big on making sure his children knew when they had done something wrong. But this time, he knew that she knew. He smiled at her, and she felt better. She had all the dishes wiped clean and on the table by the time Mother made her entrance.

"M-m-m-m, that was a good smell to wake up to," she said.

"M-m-m-m, smell bad," Tad said.

"Smells good," said Mother as she helped Tad into his booster chair.

18

Behind Mother's back, Rusty mouthed the sound-less words *Just wait* and pointed like mad towards the wastebasket. But he smiled nicely when Mother was back at her place. So did Margaret. Rusty's smile had missing teeth.

Daddy scooped two pancakes onto Mother's plate. She crooned, "This is my kind of day. What a privilege to have my happy little family pampering me. I could forget how to cook breakfast entirely if this happened more often." She gave Daddy a loving look and then reached for the strawberry jar and stopped short. Away went Margaret's smile. Rusty's grew wider. "What's this?" Mother asked.

"Margaret did it," said Rusty, grinning.

"How?" asked Mother.

"How?" asked Tad.

"Oh, Margaret's just been breaking things again," Rusty said. "She tries to balance stuff and drops it. Just like she's always done. There ought to be a rule against . . ."

Angrily, Margaret cut in. "I've set the table hundreds of times and never dropped a dish! I deserve some credit for all those perfect times!"

"How about that one week when you dropped lots of dishes every day?"

It was true that she'd dropped a few dishes the first week of intense practice of her balancing act. She said, "Practice times don't count! I hope that the next time you lie about me, Rusty, your tongue turns green!"

Tad stuck out his tongue and tried to pry open Rusty's mouth to look.

"Here we go!" shouted Daddy above Margaret's head. He scooped a pancake onto her plate, then Rusty's and Tad's. So everyone settled down to eating.

Mother said, "That's better. Let's save the arguments for another day. You can settle with me about the jar at another time, too, Margaret. Let's all act just a little more dignified at the table."

Margaret ate her pancake in silence.

Rusty ate his pancake in silence, too, but quickly. Then he asked for two more.

Margaret said she'd have two more as well. That really surprised Daddy. Breakfast was not her big meal.

Rusty said, "Make that three more."

"Make mine three," said Margaret.

Daddy gave them each three, except for Tad, who got only one. "That's the last of them," he said. "Now, no more talking until you've finished."

Mother lingered at the table. She smiled at Daddy. "So, you're leaving us again," she said. "Where are you running away to this time?"

"Not far. Sacramento. Sorry to have to be gone again with the car, but it's only for three days. Think you can hold down the fort for that long? Don't you hesitate to call a cab if you have to be somewhere. Here, let me take your dishes. Margaret, you stick around, I need to discuss something with you."

Oh no, was Daddy going to set the no-balancing rule after all?

Mother got up to leave. She scooped up Tad and marched off smiling to give him his bath. He was a three-bath-a-day kid, one after each meal.

"Well," said Daddy when he and Margaret were quite alone.

Uh, oh! When he began like that, it meant a *long* lecture or a new house rule, or both.

Margaret quickly said, "I've got two dollars and fifty cents saved to pay for Mother's jar."

"You've been saving to pay for Mother's jar? Did you *plan* to break it, Margaret?"

"I meant to say, 'I've saved two dollars and fifty cents, and you may use my savings to buy another jar.' Daddy, you know I'd never *plan* to break anything. You know that I was just practicing. . . ." She could not bring herself to say *balancing*. If he heard that word, he might make a rule against balancing. So—she would have to give up her savings for a canopy bed, but she didn't want to lose balancing, too.

"Daddy, don't make me stop balancing things. I'm very good at it. I have a *right* to do it. You yourself said that everyone has the right to be very good at something. If you make me stop balancing, then you've got to be fair and make the house rule for Rusty of no more running. It could have been him who hit Mother's jar by running too fast."

Daddy just looked at Margaret and smiled. Daddy

21

had lots of different kinds of smiles and she loved them all, except for the one he had now, an amused smile. That smile said that he was the grown-up and she was the child.

"Well, Margaret," said Daddy. "Since you were careless, I will accept the money for a new jar for your mother. That will please her, I'm sure. But look, if you and Rusty are in competition over who's the most talented, don't expect me to take sides. Now, what I wanted to tell you is I've got a surprise for you."

Caught totally off guard, Margaret whispered, "A canopy bed!"

"Well, hardly a canopy bed, kiddo. Would you settle for going to see a basketball game with your dear old dad?"

Margaret's mind came to a stop. Basketball game? It wasn't a canopy bed, but that was certainly better than a new rule. She was so relieved, she decided to be generous. "Thanks, but you can take Rusty. He really loves ball games."

"Rusty's a fine baseball player, but *you're* the one who watches basketball games on TV with me. Anyway, this game's special. I promise you, you'll like it."

She did like watching people in motion, if they weren't Rusty. It made her want to clap. But her real reason for liking TV sports was because she sat next to Daddy. "I'll go," she said.

"You won't be sorry. It's an afternoon game. I'll

22

be home at twelve thirty to pick you up. We'll grab a hamburger and go. You're in for a real surprise, I promise you. Be ready on time—that's a house rule."

Margaret Says
Too Much

Margaret was ready on time, and she did enjoy the game. The surprise was that it was a wheelchair-basketball game. Daddy told her to root for the Portland players, the men in the black shirts.

Margaret didn't root for anyone. She didn't care who won. She was amazed at the speed of the players. Man, were they fast—faster than Rusty could run! They could stop short, spin around, and dash back in another direction. It was hard just keeping track of them. "Wow!" she yelled as one man stopped so short his head went forward. A special

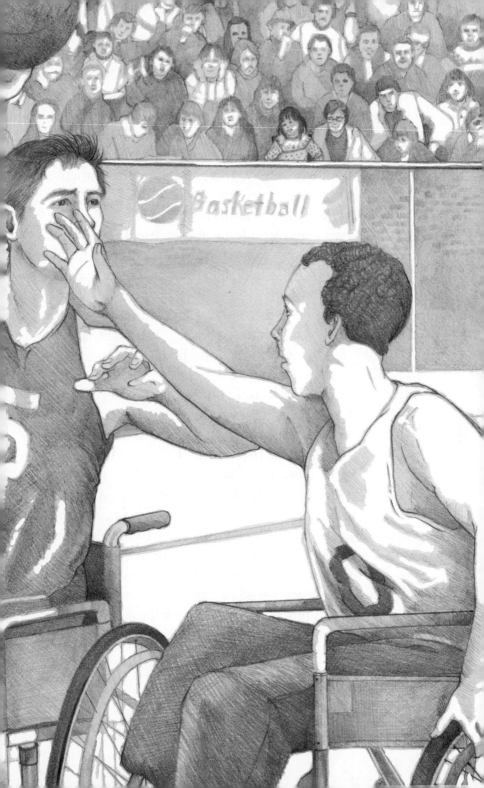

bar kept the chair from turning over. Up he came again, zipping on down the court. She clapped and clapped!

"You're rooting for the wrong team. The black shirts! The black shirts!" Daddy yelled and went on with his jumping and wiggling and popcorn munching.

Margaret's popcorn sat in her lap. She could not eat popcorn when wonders were happening before her eyes and a very important idea was forming in her mind. With a wheelchair like that, she could keep up with anyone!

When the game was over and she and Daddy were back in the car heading home, Margaret said, "Daddy, I don't want a canopy bed. . . ."

"That's good, honey. I'm relieved to hear that. I've been meaning to tell you that Dr. Sieberts told your mother and me that you must have a water bed to help keep down the pressure sores. It took so long for that last one to heal that I've been trying to budget in a way to buy that water bed for you real soon. I've even been thinking of asking your mother to release me just once from our bargain against my taking long trips. If I'd take that offer to help set up the new plant in Japan, we could buy it by the end of the summer. It'd mean I'd be gone for a couple of months, but we could certainly use the overseas bonus in a number of ways. Say, kiddo, doesn't a nice roly-poly water bed sound great?" He made motions like Groucho Marx.

She knew Daddy wished her to be happy. She

could tell by the expectant, though silly, look on his face. She tried to choose her words so she could be honest and still not make him mad. "I promise not to get any more pressure sores. I don't feel them, but I promise I'll remember to use my air cushion all the time."

Dr. Sieberts had explained to Margaret herself that because she had no feelings in her legs, she often sat in the same place too long, and the pressure stopped the blood from moving and made a sore. Margaret had an air cushion in her wheelchair that not only was soft, but allowed her to jostle about a bit more, but sometimes she forgot it if she was down on the floor with Tad.

She used her own sort of doctor's voice to explain to Daddy. "I really think I jostle around in my own bed enough while I sleep. I never wake up in the same place twice. Things will be just fine if I always use the air cushion to sit on during the day, and I cross my heart, I will."

"Good. But I think that precaution both day and . . ."

"Daddy! Please! I was going to tell you what I really wanted instead of a canopy bed. Now let me say it. Your words race ahead too fast, too. You're just like me." She put her hand out to touch Daddy's arm. The sunlight sparked off his wristwatch.

"I want a wheelchair just like the one those men use, only in my size." She pressed her head against him, waiting. But he showed no signs of excitement. His posture stayed stiff.

"Margaret, you have a fine wheelchair," he replied roughly.

"But didn't you see how they can stop, Daddy? Didn't you see how fast they got from one end of the court to the other? And the back was cut so low, I could reach way back and pick up anything I need, like a cup on the floor, or anything. No one would have to hand it to me. You know I never let kids push me, but I could if I wanted to be out in front, and sometimes I do want that. You know I *always* try to push myself."

"I know that, Margaret. Oh, honey, a wheelchair like that would cost much, much more than a canopy bed or a water bed. The water bed is a necessity. We need many things before a *sports* model. What you're asking for is a luxury."

"No! No, it's not!" She couldn't let go of this hope so quickly. She'd never let go of it. She said, "Rusty has speed."

"Margaret, let's not let the green-eyed monster of jealousy get in the way of your good sense," Daddy said in his lecture voice.

The wheelchair was not a luxury, it was . . . Oh, maybe it was wrong to have such an expensive dream. She had already accepted the fact that she couldn't do some things, but now that she had discovered that some of those things *were* possible, she wanted them. She wanted the speed and movement, the power in her own life.

"I am not asking for a toy, Daddy, I'm asking

for . . ." Her words brought new fuel to her argument. It was not nice, good fuel, but in her desperation, she used it. "Mother calls your bug-eyed monster a luxury, an expensive, broken-down toy that takes up your time and garage space besides. Why do you have that luxury?"

"Young lady, you will not speak to your father like that!" Margaret felt the whip of his words, and she knew she deserved it. She felt as if the Sprite, with its two front headlights sticking out like a bug's eyes and its parts strewn all over, were there glaring at her accusingly.

"Margaret, be reasonable! I picked up that Sprite for just two hundred dollars. It's a rare little sports car. Not many of them left in this country. When I get it fixed, it'll be worth a lot more."

She always believed that Daddy could fix anything; she didn't really doubt that he'd finish it and make money on it as he planned. But the loss of her own hope made her feel mean, and she said, "I would never let my sports model get broken down."

"Margaret! That's enough. A custom-made chair like you're talking about would cost hundreds of dollars, which we don't have. I know I have money tied up in the Sprite, and I've got to get it fixed and get the return on my investment." He paused and laughed a strange sort of laugh and said, "The longer I wait, the bigger the return on that old car, so they say." The conversation was over.

They sat in silence the rest of the way home. At

long last, they pulled into their garage alongside the bug-eyed Sprite. Daddy did not get out to bring her wheelchair around to her, as usual. He just sat there and began to talk again as if they had never stopped. "You don't know what you're asking, Margaret. It is out of the question. You've the best wheelchair we could find."

He really had not heard her at all. She hadn't complained about the quality of her chair. It was just that a different *kind* would offer her a new kind of life. She felt helpless. Suddenly she thought of a last weapon in the battle for her sports model. "I'll run away!"

"Oh, Margaret, for heaven's sake," said Daddy as he rolled down the car window.

Margaret was completely horrified at what she had said. But she repeated it again. Why? She hadn't threatened anyone like that since she was little and had told Mother she was going to jump out of the shopping cart and put back all the cereal boxes that did not have toys in them. Mother had smiled and kept on moving. Mother knew she couldn't do that. The same amused smile was on Daddy's face now.

Daddy said, "Margaret, never make a threat you're not prepared to keep."

Oh, she hated the fact that she couldn't move freely enough and fast enough to do whatever she wanted to do. "I won't be here when you get back from your trip," she muttered.

"And where would you go?" Daddy's amused

smile was growing wider. It was like when the whole family played the Super Heroes card game, and he knew just who held what card.

"I'll go to a family who will understand why I truly need a sports model," she said, and at once thought of Grandpa and Grandma.

"If you're thinking of going to your grandparents, may I warn you that the first thing they'd do is call me, and I would come and get you."

"I would not go to anyone who knew you," she said, even though something told her to stop, that the more she said, the worse trouble she'd get herself into. She turned from Daddy to look out her window to get her bearings. She saw Rusty slipping out from under the Sprite.

He stood up and demanded, "You really leaving, Margaret? Can I have your room? Boy, Tad's getting into all my things. I'd sure like to have a room of my own!"

Daddy was out of the car at once and hauling around Margaret's wheelchair. "No one's leaving. What were you doing under the Sprite, Rusty? If you're the one who lost that part to my fuel pump, I suggest you find it fast!"

Rusty smarted back, "If we got this Sprite running, then you could take it on trips, and Mother could have her own car when you're gone. I was just looking."

"Were you just looking or removing parts? Let me make it very clear to all of you, parts to this model are not replaceable! Let's get inside the house."

Now Daddy was mad at Rusty, too. Mad at both of them. Margaret knew Mother'd be in favor of the water bed and against the canopy bed and the sports-model wheelchair. So here she and Rusty were, up against their parents, and Rusty not even on her side! Not with what he had said about wanting to take over her room, wanting her gone!

Well, she'd gotten herself into a big mess, and now it looked like she'd have to leave home just to keep her dignity.

She wheeled out to the sidewalk.

"Margaret, where are you going?" Daddy demanded.

"She's running away!" Rusty shouted.

"I'm just going to the park. Rusty, when I do leave, it will be when I choose and not with you pushing me out the door!" Then she turned to Daddy and said softly, "Thanks for the basketball game."

No one tried to stop her. When she got to the park, she was glad to see Mr. Simmons on his bench.

As she drew near him, he whispered, "*Sh-h-h-h,* the ducks are coming back in. Isn't that one a beauty, Margaret?"

"Yes. I'm glad the ducks' home is in our park. I told Daddy I was leaving home. Now I've got to do it."

"Had a fight, huh? What was it about?" Mr. Simmons scooted around on the wooden slats of the park bench, letting the tail of his opened, old, gray suit coat dangle through.

"I wanted something I shouldn't want. Daddy said no, and I said I'd leave, and now I have to." Tears welled in her eyes at that awful thought, but she just sniffed real well and kept on talking until she had told him the whole story, especially the part about Daddy's calling it a luxury and also about Rusty's saying he wanted her room.

Mr. Simmons took her quite seriously and thought on it for some time. Finally, he said, "Well, Margaret, I can see your father's point. When I look at all these kids racing around here on their 3-speed and 5-speed and even 10-speed bikes, and others on roller skates so fast that they had to buy them with stop bars on the front, I think of what my wife always used to say: 'We need to slow down, stop awhile, and smell the daisies.' "

"Daisies are my favorite flowers," said Margaret. "I'd like them even if I could go real fast."

"I know, I know, child. But most grown-ups don't understand a kid's need to speed. They sorta figure it's unnecessary at best. My business partner for years said that about his son Robbie. So Robbie came to talk to me just like you're doing, Margaret. I'll tell you what I told him. One man's meat is another man's poison. If a thing's important to you, brings you happiness, no matter what the rest of the world thinks, you go ahead and work for it!"

"Did Robbie ever get what he wanted?" Margaret asked.

"Took him awhile, but he did indeed. Well, you might say he's still at it. He still comes around to discuss the matter with me, keeps me posted. You're welcome to do the same, Margaret, and I wish you luck."

Margaret thanked him and began turning her chair to go back home, but he stopped her by saying, "And another thing I might add is the light weight of those new wheelchairs. They're made of something other than that heavy stainless steel. Couple of older people I know have them, otherwise they couldn't pull the heavy weight around."

"Thanks, that makes a good argument, Mr. Simmons," Margaret said as she gave a hard tug to drag the full weight of her chair around, and then she was off. In her fantasy, she was already using her good strong arms and making her fine, lightweight sports model go zooming along.

Noodleheads

Margaret had to delay leaving home. Mother needed her help with Tad while Daddy was away. Later, when Daddy returned, he and Mother had a long serious talk and decided that, just once, Daddy must accept the offer to go overseas. The money warranted it. Margaret decided her dignity was better kept by not running away until summer was over.

Daddy handed Mother the new strawberry jar he'd gotten on the trip and said, "I appreciate you and the children being good sports about all this. Just be glad that business is as good as it is. Let's see a smile, Margaret. I don't want to see *any* long faces."

"Margaret can't smile. She's still mad," Rusty said.

"Margaret mad," said Tad and stuck out his bottom lip at her.

"Don't bother with her, Tad," said Rusty. "She's just a noodlehead who thinks she knows everything."

Margaret showed her strength by completely ignoring Rusty's remark. She went into her bedroom to study the picture she'd drawn of the sports-model wheelchair. It was hanging from the center of her curtain rod like a mobile. It was her constant reminder to work out a solution for getting that chair on her own. She was no noodlehead as Rusty had said. She would come up with something.

Mother had indeed sided with Daddy on the wheelchair issue. But she had also looked towards the garage and Daddy's own sports model sitting there amid spare parts and had lifted an eyebrow. "Mainly it's the cost," Mother explained. "If we could manage above bills, house payments, and inflation, you'd have it. I wish you *could* have it, but then you're a pretty courageous kid most of the time." She laughed, and Margaret felt reassured for a while.

If it was just a matter of money, well, she had all summer to think of ways to get enough money. If she could earn money herself to add to the overseas bonus Daddy would get, then maybe they'd have enough for the water bed and the sports model. All summer is a very long time. Even Mother agreed with that statement.

The last thing Daddy said before leaving was, "You kids help your mother, at all times, and no fighting! And Margaret, remember that it's your own responsibility to keep yourself happy."

Later, Mother didn't sound as if she was keeping herself happy when she moaned to Margaret, "Why did the overseas job have to take your father away during the summer? That's our time for visitors, and I do look forward to it, but all that cooking during the heat is not for me." She put her hand to her forehead.

No company came the first week, with the exception of Michelle. Now that they were both nine and were allowed to go the extra blocks to visit each other, they did it often. And they were busy trying to earn money.

One day Mother agreed to pay them two cents a fly for killing the flies that were swarming around on the patio. It came to twenty-eight cents for Rusty, and Margaret and Michelle each earned sixteen. Then Mother put one hand on Michelle's springy blonde curls and the other on Margaret's dark hair and said, "What do you twins plan to do next to keep yourselves occupied and happy this summer?" Michelle had asked permission to be Margaret's twin sister, and Margaret and Mother had both agreed.

"We're not doing things to keep busy, Mother. We're doing them for money. We're selling lemonade in the park, I think." Margaret looked to Michelle to confirm that. Michelle knew all about Margaret's plans for the sports model.

Michelle said, "Sure, we're selling lemonade. My mother's going to do her bookwork at one end of a picnic table, but we get to put a plastic tablecloth on the other end and run *our* business."

Mother said, "Well, I wish you luck. Make the most of your selling during the week, because I'll need Margaret at home to help me this weekend. Her grandparents are coming down."

Margaret knew that the pennies for flies and the nickels for lemonade would take a hundred years to make the hundreds of dollars needed. But she couldn't give up. As long as she was making any money at all towards her sports-model wheelchair, she felt happy. She just had to keep working at little money things until a big money-making idea came to mind. She said to Michelle, who was leaving, "You'll just love my grandparents."

Mother started walking away, too, sort of moaning again. "If only your father were here to get some of the special deli food he picks up on the way home from work. I don't want the oven to heat up the house, and I don't think his parents will be as overjoyed as you kids with macaroni and cheese!"

"Grandpa hates macaroni and cheese," Margaret and Rusty yelled together. How Grandpa could hate

Margaret and her brother's favorite meal was amazing, and when Mother cooked it so well! She always served it with hard onion bagels or soft buttery croissants and fresh diced tomatoes from her garden.

"Let's just cook outside in the cool shade of the trees every day," Margaret suggested.

Mother came back and bent to give Margaret a little hug. It felt so good. Mother was not a big hugger. "That's it!" she said. "I'll buy some special cereals for breakfast, lunch meat and fresh tomatoes should make lunch a snap, and at suppertime, you kids can get the makings from Mr. Wilet's store, and we'll let your grandpa run the cookouts. It'll give me and your grandmother a chance to really visit. I love to talk to her, and the phone is a poor substitute for a good visit. Margaret, I've always said you had a good mind." Now, Margaret really liked Mother to talk like that.

Margaret said, "Who's a noodlehead, Rusty? Mother just said I have a *good* mind!"

Michelle said, "Me, too! I have a good mind, too. I'm Margaret's twin, remember?" She went to Mother for a hug, too.

Rusty said, "I could have said that. I knew Grandpa's good at cooking out. He's always telling me about taking Daddy camping. Maybe he can help me get my cooking badge for Cub Scouts."

"Rusty, you're brilliant, too! That's a perfect idea. What am I surrounded by—the world's greatest thinkers?" Mother asked.

"Yeah!" "Yeah!" "Yeah!" they all loudly agreed, and then Rusty ran away to share that news about himself with anybody or everybody. Tad was running behind him calling, "Wait! Wait!" Margaret just smiled, feeling good.

That night for supper, Mother boiled the noodles for macaroni and cheese. Margaret slipped several long, thin spaghetti pieces in to boil, also.

"What's this?" Mother cried when she went to remove the cooked noodles.

Tad and Rusty were already at the table and had been there even as Margaret had tried to set it. They always came early for macaroni and cheese suppers. Margaret wheeled up to Mother with a bowl. "The spaghetti is for me. Put just the spaghetti strands on this plate, please. Thank you, Mother." Then she rolled back to the table while all eyes watched her, even Mother's.

She got into her own place at the table. Picking up one long strand of spaghetti with her fingers sure got Tad's attention. She made a half circle around the top of her plate. With a second strand, she completed the circle. By the time she had made two round eyes and a nose, both Rusty and Tad had caught on and were grabbing for their share of the spaghetti. At this point Mother just laughed and went back to the job of putting cheese on the macaroni. Mother didn't know that the best part was still to come.

All three had great fun making smiling mouths

and changing them to frowning mouths or yelling mouths or kissing mouths or just wiggle-waggle mouths like most of Tad's were.

Mother said, "Enough! Let's clean up the plates. Your food is ready." She set the bowl of macaroni and cheese on the table. Rusty was getting up to dump his plate of spaghetti art into the sink.

"Hold it!" sang Margaret. "Now comes the really best part."

Rusty stopped and looked back.

Margaret scooped up a huge glob of macaroni and cheese from the bowl and loudly but slowly said, "Here goes old"—then, very quickly as she dumped it—"macaroni and cheese in the face!"

Rusty yelled, "Hey, that's neat!" and he was back at once and gave his plate a faceful.

Tad screeched, "Roni-sheez!" and dump, dump, his plate was full.

They all had second faces and second facefuls. Rusty said, "That was really good thinking, Margaret." Then he had thirds.

No one ate the bagels or croissants except for Mother. That's all she ate. She said they could have all the cheese and noodles if they wished, and added, "I think I'm spending this summer with a bunch of noodleheads."

Margaret didn't mind at all Mother's saying that. She sounded so happy. Mother had a hard time being this happy when Daddy was gone. Margaret knew then that she'd kept her promise to Daddy and had been a good sport and brought cheer to herself and to her family. To top it off, Rusty had complimented her! It was a wonderful feeling!

The feeling got even better the next day when Grandpa and Grandma came. Margaret sneaked up behind their backs while Mother was telling them of the planned cookouts—Margaret's idea. Mother went on to tell them how clever Margaret was to have invented the spaghetti faces and how the kids had loved it.

"That Margaret," said Grandma. "Sometimes I just wonder what's hiding behind those sparkling eyes of hers."

Grandpa said, "Yep, she's quite a girl."

Wow! It was good to hear people saying nice things about you, behind your back, so to speak. And the same noodlehead that had thought up that terrific fun game could surely think up a way to get herself a sports-model wheelchair, too!

Onionheads

Grandma and Grandpa took naps the afternoon of their arrival. They'd gotten up way before daybreak to make the long drive down from Seattle. While Margaret waited for them to wake up, she perfected a few balancing tricks to show them. Mother was too busy to notice. She was sitting at the kitchen table addressing letters to leaders in the spina-bifida organization. She was the national secretary this year.

Margaret was keeping an eye on Tad while she

practiced balancing a lunch box on her head. Rusty stuck out a finger and tipped it, forcing her to catch it and start over.

"Your lunch box is supposed to be stored away for the summer," Rusty said. "You want to break your thermos again?"

"This practice is to *keep* from breaking my thermos again. My thermos *is* safely stored away. Next, I'll try it with food in it and when I'm perfect, I'll do it with my thermos in it, too." She then balanced the lunch box perfectly and held it steady, even while turning her wheelchair around. Did Rusty notice that? Nope, he just noticed when things went wrong.

At least one person in the family noticed how good she was. Tad clapped for her. She let him try to balance her lunch box on his head, but it ended in such a banging racket that Mother yelled, "Into the family room, Margaret! Your grandparents are trying to sleep, and I can't hear myself think with all that noise."

So she put away her lunch box and balanced blocks for Tad into great towers. He danced and clapped like mad. "See?" Margaret called to Rusty, who was whipping his little Matchbox sports-cars across the family-room floor, trying to knock down the tower. "Tad appreciates my balancing."

"Tad's two. Big deal," Rusty said.

"Two or not, he knows something good when he sees it."

"See it! See it!" yelled Tad. "Now, Margaret?"

Margaret made her finger and thumb touch to make an *O*, which was the signal for Tad to punch. Wow! Her little brother had a good left punch and could smash a tower flat in a split second. She *rah-rah-rah*ed for him, and she and Tad were so happy that Rusty left for outside.

Rusty was soon back, banging the door loudly as he came in. He couldn't get his baseball cap down from the garage rafters where Daddy had tossed it when he'd found it lying under the hood of the Sprite. Rusty deserved it for messing with the Sprite again just after Daddy had told him it was off-limits.

Margaret said, "*Sh-h-h-h!* Don't wake up Grandpa and Grandma. I'll think of a way to get it for you, Rusty." She went with him to the garage. A garden hoe was too short to reach. Neither Rusty nor she could manage the big extension ladder. There was simply no way for Rusty to crawl up. She saw on the floor of the garage something that might help.

"Up there, dummy, my cap's up there."

"Don't you ever call me that again, Rusty! You want your cap or not?"

"Yeah, I'm sorry, okay?"

Margaret reached for the long, thin strip of wood that lay on the floor. Daddy had it leftover from fixing a trellis on the patio. It would do fine.

She couldn't quite reach down to it because her wheelchair was too high. Wouldn't the sports model, which was built low for such reaching, come in handy now? However, she didn't have the sports model yet, so she had to ask Rusty to hand the thin strip of wood to her. The wood was pretty wobbly, bending this way and that as she tried to reach Rusty's cap.

Rusty grabbed it from her, and it wobbled even more for him, because he was in such a hurry. Finally he just used it for a whacking stick which wedged the cap all the more. "Darn Daddy! How'd he like me to throw his baseball cap up there?"

"Give me the trellis wood, Rusty. Daddy doesn't have a baseball cap, and you know it. Don't touch me. Easy does it." Very carefully, very slowly, she found the balance to the stick and then moved it straight up, and then one quick flip up and aside, and Rusty's cap was perched neatly on top of the wood stick.

Was he impressed? No way. Did he say thank you? No way. What Rusty did say was, "Last thing Daddy said was that his tools and lumber are off-limits. You'd better not let him catch you using his lumber. I could have done that in the first place if I'd wanted to use his lumber."

This was not like the good old days, after all. Rusty was off to the vacant lot without her. He was pretty speedy. But speed hadn't gotten him his baseball cap, had it? No, just his baseball glove. Oh, she shouldn't have remembered that. She'd promised Daddy that she wouldn't fight or be jealous. But all summer was so long. She guessed that it'd take something really super to impress Rusty anymore. Maybe a really great balancing feat would win Rusty over. It couldn't be some simple thing like getting his ball cap. No, it'd have to be a really big important, maybe dangerous thing. She would save Rusty's life, that's what she'd do.

Rusty would be out playing on the vacant lot and would hurt his foot so badly that he'd be lying on the ground, stiff with pain. She'd come to his rescue, snatch him up, balance him on one hand like a waiter balancing those large trays, and wheel him on back home to safety—and the cheers of her neighbors and family. And when Rusty got better, he'd be cheering for her, too, forever and ever! She might even forget her good friend, Michelle, and Rusty might even forget all the guys he played baseball with and . . .

"Margaret!" Mother was calling.

"I'm coming. I'm coming." Margaret went back inside, and there were Grandma and Grandpa. Tad was pouting. Mother said, "Margaret, I thought I told you to keep an eye on Tad. Now he's gone and wakened your grandparents."

"Wake up!" shouted Tad and stamped his foot and then began to really bawl.

Grandma swept him up in her arms and said, "It's okay, Taddy, we needed to wake up anyway. Grandpa's got to get the fire going and our suppers cooked."

Mother frowned.

Margaret quickly pulled Grandpa towards the door. "Come on outside, Grandpa. I'll show you where the grill is." She was proud of it. It was one she'd made herself by carefully alternating and stacking bricks until it met city standards for open campfires.

From far over on the vacant lot, Rusty spotted Grandpa and was yelling for him to come watch him play baseball. Grandpa stood as if thinking it over for a minute, watching Rusty play from where he stood. Then he gave a whistle and said, "I'll say, that grandson of mine is something!" and off he went.

Well, that made about the four-hundred-and-fifty-millionth time Margaret had heard what a great baseball player Rusty was. Margaret had no options but to sit and seethe and wait until Grandpa returned.

Grandpa tapped Margaret on the head and said, "Come along, Margaret. Let's run over to Mr. Wilet's Convenient. Company's no good unless they add a few spices to the pot. You come, too, Rusty. I need both of you onionheads to help me. You're lucky to have a store at the end of your block. Most of those stores are gone nowadays."

"Don't walk so fast, Grandpa. One day I'm going to get me a sports-model wheelchair, and then I can go to the store as fast as you and Rusty. No! NO! Don't push me. I can push myself! I just wanted you not to go so fast."

"She just wanted you to know she's going to buy

herself a real sports model, so she thinks," said Rusty. "Mother and Daddy say she doesn't have to have a sports model. She probably won't get it 'cause it costs so much. We better slow down for her, Grandpa. It's okay if we walk slow. Sometimes I walk slow when I want to. Nobody can eat until we get back anyway."

"No truer words were ever spoken," Grandpa said and put his arm around Rusty's shoulder, but Rusty broke loose after a while in order to be the first one inside the store.

What Grandpa bought was not spices. It was two big red onions, and he named one of them Rusty and the other Margaret as he picked them out.

Margaret said, "My hair's black, Grandpa, not red."

Grandpa stuck an onion up against Margaret's hair and said, "You're right. Doesn't match." Then he stuck the other onion up to Rusty's hair and said, "Not an exact match either. We'll just have to add a little purple dye to your hair color to get the onion shade of red, Rusty. Remember that, the next head-washing. Well, do we keep the unmatched onions or not? Okay! Okay! Margaret, you hang on to them."

Margaret did more than hang on, she tried to balance them. But they were pretty round, and one almost got away, so she had to be careful.

Grandpa handed Rusty a half gallon of dill pickles to carry. "Well, that ought to do it unless you don't have any mustard at home," he said.

"Mother's got a whole year's supply of mustard," said Margaret. "Mustard lasts forever, especially the kind with horseradish in it."

When they got back, Rusty and Grandpa began collecting firewood to build a fire. Margaret told Mother and Grandma just to keep Tad out of her way, so she could slice the onions and pat out the hamburgers. She wasn't finished yet when Rusty called that the fire was ready. She ignored him until she did finish and could anchor the things firmly in her lap to get them out to him.

"What took you so long? Can't you even hurry when Grandpa's waiting? By the time they're done, it will be Christmas," Rusty grumbled.

Actually, things were ready to eat by six o'clock, which was perfect timing. Those hamburgers, cooked on an open fire, were so good that Mother said they'd have to have company picnics like this all summer.

Two days later, after Grandma and Grandpa went home, Aunt Patty and her boyfriend, Scott, came over from Reed College, where they were going to summer college. They didn't call first, just dropped by. Mother immediately asked Rusty and Margaret to go to the store for picnic supplies. Rusty took off at once, calling back to Margaret, "You coming? Well, then move faster. Use your muscles."

She did move pretty fast. They were to buy the same picnic stuff they'd had before. Mother said that

51

there was no use in changing a winning menu. Besides, it was festive and economical and foolproof. Margaret appreciated all those big words, for the picnic idea had been hers.

Of course, Rusty already had the hamburger meat and buns in the cart by the time Margaret got inside the store. He said, "Get the onions, Margaret, while I get the pickles. And get a move on. Aunt Patty's friend will starve waiting."

Margaret refused to hurry. She had to straighten up the onion bin. It was a mess.

Lots of things in Mr. Wilet's store were a mess. She'd straightened up things before when she and Mother had shopped there. Rusty would just have to wait for her. She had the money, and he couldn't check out without her. She finished things off quite nicely. The onions looked neat, but Rusty didn't say anything about them.

Rusty beat her home, of course. Tad's bouncy ball was laid aside, and Scott was helping Rusty build the fire. Scott said, "I'm an old Boy Scout from way back. See, you lay the first layer of sticks like this, and next we'll . . ." Margaret went inside to see Aunt Patty.

Aunt Patty was helping Mother shape the hamburgers. She said, "I'm an experienced hasher, Margaret, you know that? That's how I earn college money, working in the college cafeteria. Terrific talent to have on campus."

"I have a talent," said Margaret. She immediately

showed Aunt Patty how she could balance the two onions. Oops, it slipped. Rusty noticed that, of course, and laughed. "Onions are hard to balance!" yelled Margaret. It took five tries and four spills, but she did it!

"You've a terrific talent there, kid," said Aunt Patty. "Now, if you can slice them as well, you're sure to get a job on campus when you go to college." So Margaret sliced the onions. Everybody hurrayed for that, even Rusty, but mostly because they were all ready to start eating.

Anyway, Margaret took Rusty's hurrays as being for her balancing trick and not just because of the onions being ready. If he only knew it, that balancing trick was the most important one she'd ever done, by far. If she could balance vegetables, then she had a great new idea of how to earn lots of money, really big money, this summer. And she'd not have to wait until she started college to get a job, either. The sports-model wheelchair was practically hers! This good old onionhead of hers had not let her down. She could hardly wait to report her plan to Mr. Simmons.

Like the Good Old Days

On Friday of that week, Mother hung up the phone to announce that Grandpa and Grandma were coming down from Seattle again. "Your father has written to them. I just know it. He's asked them to check on us. I'll bet you anything! Their excuse was that they had to pick up your Aunt Patty at college on their way back home. But last week Patty told me she had a ride home with a friend."

Tad was dancing around happily and Rusty was joining in. Margaret frowned. "Don't you want Grandpa and Grandma to come?"

"Of course, I like to see them, same as you, but it's the cost. They're not exactly rich, you know? Sometimes your father forgets they're on a fixed income when he asks favors, and they'd never say no to your father."

"Oh," said Margaret and felt *very* happy. She did love her grandparents, but also it would mean another trip to the store, and this time she was going to apply for a job! Mr. Simmons even believed she would get it.

Rusty said, "Mother, how is it that Daddy can say no to us when Grandpa can't say no to him?" Margaret wished that she had asked that. She was certainly going to discuss the business of Daddy's saying no to the sports model with him when he got home. And if she got this job and had money to hand to him along with that discussion—well, who knows?

Mother said, "Oh, he'll probably be the same way with you kids when he gets older."

"Why wait?" asked Rusty.

"Yeah, why wait?" said Margaret and joined in the laughter with her brothers.

Mother said, "All right, cut it out. Looks like we're in for another picnic. I did insist that they come down later in the day this time. Why don't we have everything ready for the picnic when they get down here? I don't want them to have to pay for it, and it'll show them that we're doing just fine on our own." That was certainly okay with Margaret. It'd be best not to have others around during her job interview. She'd have to wear her best blouse, the daisy one.

When Rusty and Margaret got to Mr. Wilet's Convenient the next day, they felt just like Daddy when he said he got caught in rush-hour traffic. There were plenty of others around. It was no time to ask for a job. In fact, the place was swarming with people. Hands were grabbing things from the shallow vegetable bins so fast that Margaret couldn't tell which hand belonged to what person. Onions, celery, lettuce. Grab! Grab! Grab! Hands going over the top of her. Hands moving in from the side of her. All this stuff they put into carts. The aisles were full of carts. Carts bumping into her wheelchair, locking their wheels to hers. She looked to Rusty for help. He had noticed and had come back to her.

Rusty said, "Margaret, you want me to get the onions, and you get the pickles?"

She knew Rusty meant well, and she was thankful he'd pulled her back and away, but she said, "Nope, I'll do it. You go on and get your pickles."

"Have it your way," he said. "But don't waste time on straightening the bin this time, or Grandpa and Grandma'll be here before we get back." He rushed his cart towards the canned goods to get the pickles. He rushed his cart just a little too fast. He pushed over a stack of canned beans that were on special.

Worse yet, when he tried to get his cart back out, he bumped into someone else, who in turn bumped into a display of oranges. The oranges rolled all over the floor. Mr. Wilet was there at once, and he

wasn't very happy about having all his merchandise lying in a big mess on the floor.

Rusty was down on the floor now, too, and was handing up cans of beans to Margaret. "Here, quick, help me clean this up. You know how to stack things. Hurry! Hurry! Grandpa will beat us home!" He moaned.

Mr. Wilet had dashed back to the cash register to check out the people in line. "What a day to be running a one-man store," he said.

Margaret said to Rusty, "I won't hurry. You cannot mix hurry and balancing. I learned that when Mother's strawberry jar got broken. Mother will just have to hold down the fort until we get home."

Anyone could easily tell that Rusty was mad at her for being so slow. His face showed red pretty fast when he was mad. But he had no choice, so he kept handing her things one at a time. She put the cans of beans on their stand in eight neat columns, nicely balanced with the different brand labels, blacks and reds, showing in the front like a giant checkerboard. People began to admire it—even Rusty.

Next Rusty tackled getting the oranges to her. This took a bit of running, so he was happy, and she was able to keep up with him very well. She built a beautiful pyramid of them. It looked much better than the mess that Mr. Wilet had in his original display.

When Mr. Wilet finally got time to look up and see the marvelous display, he came out and fairly danced around it. "I say! That's a beautiful, sumptuous job of balancing! Don't know that my oranges have ever looked that nice, even when they were on the tree!"

Now was the perfect time for Margaret to say what she had planned to say at the job interview. "I could balance all your vegetables! I could make everything in your store look this pretty! I could have a job with you, balancing things. You could pay me for it."

Rusty wasted no time in catching on to her job request. He said, "Me, too. I'll hand her the things. You could pay me, too." Looked as if Rusty had forgotten about wanting to get home in a hurry.

Mr. Wilet wiped his hands across the big apron that he had wrapped around his thin body. "You two kids are some hustlers, ain't you? I'll bet you knocked those displays down on purpose."

"No, honest, cross my heart," Rusty was saying.

"Rusty would *never* do such a thing! He may push his cart too fast, and he may yell sometimes, but he's not like *that*. It was an accident. Besides, I was going to ask you for a job anyway. Even without the spills. Didn't you notice how I fixed up your onion bin the other day?"

"You did that? I was selling so many red onions all of a sudden, I had to come back and check out why. Well, I don't know. Give me time to think about it. Look, I got people to check through right now." Mr. Wilet went back to the cash register. Already people were buying beans and oranges.

When Rusty and Margaret had their turn checking out their picnic stuff, Mr. Wilet said, "Well, I guess I could let you have a little off on this bill for fixing up things so nice, but you kids are a little young to be out-and-out hired. Besides, my helper is coming back from vacation in two days."

"No," said Margaret. "We can't be paid for today. Rusty knocked the stuff down, and if anyone should pay me, it would have to be him. I . . . ."

"No way!" said Rusty, backing off. "I'm not paying you, Margaret. I don't pay my own sister for anything!"

"As I was saying," continued Margaret, "I-I'd do any balancing job for you for a-a . . . a dollar." She hated to say such a big amount, but it was going to take lots of dollars for the sports model.

"Me, too. A dollar! I could have things out of the bins in a hurry and hand them to Margaret to balance. My sister is very, very good when it comes to balancing things. Why, there's nothing in this world that she can't balance." Margaret couldn't believe she was hearing Rusty say all that! And he was still talking. He was saying, "I'm eight and a half, and she's nine and a half, and that makes eighteen, and that's old enough to get a job."

Margaret could do nothing but nod in agreement. She didn't remember when she'd agreed with Rusty so much, and all at once, too. Why, it *was* like the good old days.

Mr. Wilet was scratching his head. He said, "You kids sure do like to drive a hard bargain. I just don't think . . ."

Rusty cut in, "You did see that perfect job Margaret did? It looked better to me than anything I've seen in the biggest supermarkets. Why, I've a good mind to go knock down those oranges again just to see Margaret balance them up again. We would help you keep your store looking great. And you know I'm fast, really fast. Just ask Margaret."

"Yep, he is!" Margaret said and kept nodding her head, but keeping her eye on Mr. Wilet's face.

"Hey, this is what I call two against one. I don't stand a chance. You kids are all right. Most kids who come in here shopping with their mothers couldn't be concerned about the trouble they cause me. You sort of make me believe in kids again. Both of you! And it's a pure pleasure to see a brother and sister admiring and caring for each other the way you two do." Mr. Wilet paused to look them over.

Margaret felt all warm and excited. She was glad she'd worn her blouse with the daisies on it. She'd thought it would be best for the job interview. Rusty's ears had turned red from all the praise.

Mr. Wilet finally spoke. "A dollar a bin, I'll pay. You want two dollars, that'll mean two bins. That understood?"

Neither of them could answer, but two heads nodded.

"And I'll expect you here after a rush day like today. Happens every weekend. Things sort of go down the drain after a real stampede like today. Okay if you start work this Monday, then come again on Friday to make sure things are looking good for the weekend?"

Rusty managed a grunt, and Margaret just nodded some more.

"Think your parents will go along with all this?"

Now Margaret could speak. "I'm sure they'll be delighted," she said.

That settled, they paid for their picnic supplies and headed back home. Probably Grandma and Grandpa were already there. But what a reason Margaret and Rusty had to tell for being late!

Rusty got there first, of course, and got to tell it all to Grandpa and Grandma and Mother. There they were, all standing in the yard watching Margaret approach. She didn't mind being behind. It gave her time to figure out how many dollars she'd have by the end of summer and dream of how fast she would speed home from the store in her sports model.

Now, she moved very slowly, balancing both the hamburger meat and the buns on top of her head. Tad was jumping up and down and clapping. Grandpa was laughing. Grandma was smiling and saying something Margaret could barely hear. "To think their father was worried about them. Wait'll he hears they got themselves a job. Think you kids can handle it?"

"Sure!" sang Margaret.

"Sure," said Rusty.

"They'll do fine. We'll all do just fine," said Mother.

Grandpa and Grandma simply nodded, and Margaret knew that the next time they came it would be just to visit. She also knew that what had once seemed almost impossible—that Rusty would be her partner again—had happened. Getting a sports model should be easy by comparison.

Summer and Business Expansion

Margaret and Rusty did work very well together in Mr. Wilet's store. Sometimes they did two bins, sometimes three or four for Mr. Wilet. And Mr. Wilet always made sure he paid them in crisp dollar bills, which felt really good in their hands. It felt like big business, but still it was not enough. Rusty was interested in the new soccer-ball field being set up in the park and not in extra jobs. Margaret made endless pages of calculations. What she needed to know was just exactly how much a sports model would cost. Mother refused to call a salesroom to find out.

"Margaret, you might as well make other plans for your money," she said. "The bulk of your father's bonus is going towards the purchase of your water bed. This conversation is ended."

"But Mother, I haven't got a single pressure sore since I've started using my air cushion *all* the time. Anyway, I never wanted a water bed. All I've wanted was a canopy bed, and now I'm even giving that up, too, in favor of my sports model."

"Boy, I'd like a water bed," said Rusty. "You could jump on it and roll on it and plop on it!"

"Rusty, I don't jump. Dr. Sieberts wants me to have it so I sort of sink into it with even weight from all my body. I'm supposed to feel like I'm floating on a cloud. I'll just lie easy on my regular bed. I'd rather have motion and speed than floating."

"I might buy a water bed," said Rusty. "Well, after I get a new case for my Matchbox cars and some roller skates with stop bars and . . . Well, I used to want a bigger baseball glove, 'cause the glove I won is just a toy, but now I want a soccer ball. I'm going to get a real one, and then I might get . . ."

Mother said, "Enough, Rusty! How many weeks do you think are in a summer? And Margaret, you could stand to make a few other plans. You *will* be getting the water bed. Let's not hear another word about the sports model. Do you know your father is going to be a very surprised man when he hears about your jobs. I haven't mentioned one word when he's called."

"Snort, snort," sang Tad.

"Sports model," corrected Margaret, saying the words in spite of Mother's warning, as if those words repeated often would make her dream happen.

"Margaret!" scolded Mother. "*You* might practice being a good sport for a change."

"I'm sorry," said Margaret, and she was. She knew it was her responsibility to see to her own happiness. Daddy had said so. And Mr. Simmons had told her that it was very nice of her parents to want to get things for her that she needed.

"I guess I'll go hang out at the park with Michelle," said Margaret, and headed for the door. Rusty raced off ahead of her.

"Park! Wait! Wait!" yelled Tad.

Mother picked up Tad and said, "Oh, my Taddy Baby, don't you know that your brother and sister are growing older and are leaving us for interests of their own? You and I will play in the backyard. Margaret, be home by lunch."

Margaret rolled on out the door, leaving behind the sounds of her little brother's shouts.

For a long moment, sadness filled her. Mother's words were true. She and Rusty were both leaving the house, but not together. They were separate. Only for the short time working at Mr. Wilet's store

were they ever together anymore. Rusty had interests. Margaret had interests. But it was Michelle,
not Rusty, who shared Margaret's interests. She
guessed it was all right. She moved as fast as her
wheelchair would go, headed straight for the park.

Michelle was still inside her house, so Margaret
went as far as the front steps and yelled for her.
Michelle came out and opened the yard gate at the
side of the house so Margaret could roll in through
the big patio doors around back, which were at
ground level.

"Guess what?" said Michelle. "Mother's going to
make stuff for a party. You want to see what I can
do with the soft cheese?"

"I guess so," said Margaret.

So Michelle filled her mouth full of soft orange
cheese and then clopped it closed, holding her lips
apart so her teeth would show. Bits of orange cheese
oozed out through spaces on each side where Michelle had lost baby teeth. Now it looked as if she
had fangs.

"My turn," shouted Margaret, and soon she, too,
wore orange fangs. They stood and stared at each
other until the giggles mixed with their mouthfuls of
cheese and made them choke. They gulped it all
down, and did it again. And again, and again, until
all of Michelle's mother's party cheese was gone.

"We're going to get into trouble," whispered
Margaret.

"No," said Michelle with a sigh. "My mother never scolds me."

"Wow, are you lucky! Why doesn't she ever scold you?"

Michelle tiptoed to the other room to make sure her mother was busy at her books, and then she came back and whispered, "Because I'm an only child and because . . ." Michelle waited so very long to finish that Margaret thought maybe some cheese or something was hung in her throat. At last, she said the rest. ". . . because she doesn't love me."

"Michelle, you've got to be wrong!" Margaret couldn't help but say that pretty loud. "She doesn't scold you because she *does* love you a lot. I wish my parents loved me that much. I got scolded this morning for talking about getting my sports-model wheelchair. Michelle, I've just got to earn lots more money so I can buy it myself."

"Margaret, I'll help you earn the money if you promise me that you'll be my twin forever and ever. Do you promise?"

"Why do I have to promise that? If we're twins, we're twins, that's all. Anyway, I promise." Margaret drew a big cross over her chest. "You don't have to give me your share of the money. Rusty keeps his money, and I keep mine. So you keep yours. What are we going to do? We only made twenty cents on the lemonade. I really need dollars, lots of dollars."

"I do have to give you my share, 'cause you need it. I want you to always be my friend."

"Well, you don't have to pay me for that! Friends don't have to pay friends to be friends." Margaret yelled that so loudly that Michelle's mother came running in.

Before her mother could question them, Michelle said a strange thing. She said, "Margaret and I are going to be a sextet."

Now Michelle's mother got that awful, amused adult smile on her face. She said, "Well, that's good, dear. I'm curious as to just how the two of you can pull that off."

"We'll just charge people in the park to hear us sing. Your group gets paid, so our group will, too." Margaret knew that Michelle's mother did the booking for a singing group. Margaret also knew that Michelle was trying to out-argue her mother just as she had to out-argue her own parents at times. They surely were twins all right. Michelle had thought really fast to make such an announcement to her mother to cover for Margaret having yelled. But what a thing to think of! If they really could earn money just for singing in the park, well . . .

Michelle's mother said, "Well, I'll leave this group of two to tend to their business while I get back to my own business."

"We'll be in the park singing," said Michelle.

As soon as they got out of the house and could speak freely, Margaret said, "You're a real fast-thinking twin to think that up. Who are we going to sing to, and how do we get them to pay? Michelle,

I think sextet is more than two people. I think that's why your mother smiled like that. I really hate it when grown-ups smile like that, don't you?"

"Oh, she does that all the time. I told you, she doesn't love me. I told you, she never, never scolds me, and that proves it. All right, we'll get the Bernstein twins to join us, and then we'll be a sextet." Michelle headed over towards the next block right away. Margaret followed.

The Bernstein twins couldn't come because they were having to help their mother with a yard sale. They loved yard sales and had them at the beginning and end of every summer, and sometimes in between. They did promise to join the sextet, for they loved to sing "On Top of Spaghetti." So that much got settled.

Michelle and Margaret stuck around while looking over all the things for sale. There was two of everything. Then Margaret saw them—two of the most beautiful white sundresses all trimmed in embroidered yellow daisies! The price tag said 50¢. For one crisp dollar bill, she and Michelle could have those dresses.

"Michelle, stand right by these dresses, and don't let anyone buy them until I get back."

"Oh, I love them," cried Michelle. "My mother would never buy it for me. She won't let me buy things at yard sales."

"I have my own dollar," said Margaret. "I can buy them myself. My mother doesn't have to let me. Stay right with them and hold on!"

Margaret really wished she had a sports model to speed home in, but anyway she got there and back as fast as she could and handed the crisp dollar bill to Mrs. Bernstein.

Mrs. Bernstein said, "Well, do you want them in a bag or would you like to wear them home?"

"Oh, could we?" shouted Margaret and Michelle.

Mrs. Bernstein let them use the breezeway between their garage and house to do their changing. Then she put their old clothes in two bags and told them, "Thanks, kids, and good-bye. Just where are you going all dressed up?"

"To the park to sing," answered Michelle, as if it had been a part of their plan to get these dresses for singing all along.

Once in the park, when they stopped for further plans, Margaret asked, "Do you think your mother will let you keep the dress?"

"Of course she will, if you gave it to me. But Margaret, I'll pay you back, okay? I even look like your twin now." She swung around, making the skirt fly out.

"I know," said Margaret, equally pleased.

"Margaret, have you ever wondered why our names both begin with M? You know what I think? I think we were meant to be twins from the day we were born. Let's go find somebody to sing to."

"First we've got to decide what to sing," said Margaret.

" 'The Star Spangled Banner,' of course," said Michelle, pointing now towards Mr. Simmons, who was sitting on the park bench watching ducks float by.

Boy, Michelle was fast to think up things and even faster to put them into action. Margaret didn't have much time to be scared about the whole thing. She just moved along with Michelle, and when they got right in front of Mr. Simmons, Michelle said, "Now, Margaret! 'Oh, say can you see . . .' "

Margaret joined right in and, there, they had done it: sung their first song for money.

Mr. Simmons said, "Well, Michelle and Margaret, what's this all about?"

"We were just singing," said Margaret.

"So you were, and very pretty, too. Those daisy dresses you're wearing are pretty as well. Why did you pick 'The Star Spangled Banner' to sing to me?"

"Because you were sitting here," said Michelle.

"But you don't usually sing that song unless there's an occasion. Doesn't really matter, though— you were good performers. And performers deserve to be paid. Here, here, let me find some change, give you something for that fine show you put on for me."

Then, for some very strange and unknown reason, Margaret heard herself saying, "No, Mr. Simmons. We just did it for you for nothing. We like to sing 'The Star Spangled Banner.' You don't have to pay us for singing."

Then, as if she were Margaret's true twin, Michelle whispered, "Of course not. You don't ever

have to pay a friend to be a friend." They waved at Mr. Simmons and left him sitting there all pleased and smiling at the sun. And Margaret felt her own happiness swelling to near bursting.

They sang to each other for a while and then sang to some ducks under the bridge in the Japanese garden. And then Margaret's stomach told her it was time for macaroni and cheese, and she went home.

She had to explain to her family about the new dress and how it was to make her part of a sextet and to help her earn money by singing, so that maybe she could buy . . . She didn't say *sports model,* she said, "Buy something."

"Sextet?" asked Mother. "Just the *two* of you are a sextet?"

"Well," said Rusty, "did you earn any money?"

"No, I just spent a dollar," Margaret said.

"That's really saving fast," mocked Rusty.

Mother said, "Leave her alone, Rusty. You go play somewhere else now."

Margaret knew that Mother was being understanding. She appreciated that, although she didn't really need to be understood right now.

Very quietly, she turned her back on Rusty and went to find her songbook. She thought she'd like to learn the second verse of "The Star Spangled Banner." Wouldn't that be a nice surprise for Mr. Simmons? As for money and business expansion— well, she and Michelle would come up with something.

The Water Bed
Trade-off

Summer was about over, and Daddy would be home very soon.

Margaret and Michelle had found a way to make some good money with their singing, but not nearly enough for the sports model. But hope came when Mother remarked that Daddy's overseas bonus was going to be substantial. Now, all Margaret had to do was persuade him to skip buying the water bed. With his bonus added to her money, they'd surely have enough to buy the sports model. After all, she had twenty-six crisp dollar bills plus an extra 50 cents from Mr. Wilet. That's a lot of money! Also, she had $6.80 in her secret pencil box made like a giant pencil. That money she had earned killing flies, 2 cents each; lemonade, 5 cents a glass; and the rest from singing. The grand total was $33.30.

At first the singing had all been for free, even after the Bernstein twins had joined the sextet and really did a great job with "On Top of Spaghetti." What made it start paying off was the weddings. There had been three summer weddings held in the little Japanese garden at the end of the park. Then it didn't matter if they sang "The Star Spangled Banner" or "On Top of Spaghetti" or "Row, Row, Row Your Boat," people tossed coins to them. Yep, there was real money to be made in weddings. Just walk around the park among the wedding guests before or after the ceremony and sing, and you'd get paid.

Margaret was counting all her money and telling all this to Grandpa and Grandma. They had come to stay with Margaret and Rusty and Tad while Mother was away at the spina-bifida convention. She was meeting Daddy there. They listened to her carefully and seemed excited for her. Then Grandma whispered something to Grandpa and went to the phone to call Aunt Patty. Grandma talked to Aunt Patty an awfully long time, long-distance. But by the time she was finished, even from hearing only one side of the conversation, Margaret already knew the news, the real reason they were so excited.

When Grandma hung up, Margaret shouted it

out. "Aunt Patty is going to marry Scott in our little Japanese garden! Hurray! Hurray!"

Tad came in off the back patio and shouted, "Hurray! Hurray!"

"Oh, Tad, you don't know what you're yelling for. Aunt Patty is getting married. Then her Scott will be our Uncle Scott. How about that?"

"Hurray, hurray!"

Then Grandma said, "Margaret, we have you to thank for finding the place. Anyway, Scott had wanted it down here. You know, he lives only about ten miles from you. And now all their friends from Reed College can come. This will work well. A park wedding. Margaret, what a nice thing you've done for your family. We can handle the wedding right from your house if your parents say yes."

"I'm absolutely positively certain that they will," said Margaret.

"And you kids could be in the wedding. Patty's already said she wanted Margaret for flower girl and Rusty for ring bearer."

Margaret loved the idea, but Rusty said, "No way! I saw one of those weddings in the park. We stopped our soccer game to look over the fence into the Japanese garden. Some little kid dressed in a funny suit was carrying the rings on a pillow. I'm not little, I'm eight! And I'm not dressing like that. Count me out! And what if we have a game that day? Then I couldn't be in the wedding anyway!"

Rusty was talking about his all-important soccer game. That was the new thing for him, and he had already spent a lot of his earnings from Mr. Wilet to buy his own real soccer ball. Even more than baseball, soccer games were lots of running, running. The field where they played was just on the other side of the Japanese garden. But no way would Mother allow him to miss the wedding for a soccer game. He'd be there even if he had no part in it.

Normally, Margaret would have thought Rusty was wrong about not wanting to be a part of the wedding, but she herself had watched three weddings, and all the ring bearers were little boys about four years old. Their suits were cute, not funny. "Rusty's too old," said Margaret. "Better use him to set up chairs. There are always three rows of chairs set up in front of Mr. Simmons' park bench, where he sits to watch ducks glide under the curved bridge. If it's a wedding, he watches that instead. The part he likes best is when the bride walks over the bridge to her groom. Michelle and I always sit beside Mr. Simmons and watch while the weddings are going on. Then we sing for the guests after. Mr. Simmons says we add to his change of scenery. He's very nice."

Grandma patted Margaret's arm and said, "We'll use you as a consultant on how things are done."

Grandma went on. "My, this trip down here to do your parents a favor has turned out to be a very big favor for us. You really don't know how much you've helped us, Margaret. I hope I get a chance to return your favor someday." Margaret thought she might use her as a consultant on getting a good argument to sway Daddy.

Grandpa was down crawling around on the family-room floor, being a horse for Tad. Just then, he bucked Tad off and then scooped him up to stand him up straight and announced, "Here's your ring bearer!"

Both Margaret and Rusty shouted, "Not Tad!"

But Grandma and Grandpa went on talking as if that made the best sense in the world. They even got on the phone again and talked to Aunt Patty about it. Grandma said, "He'd look adorable. All he'd have to do is walk behind his sister. The rings will be hooked on, so what does it matter that he's just two?"

Margaret knew that it mattered, but they were going to do it anyway, so why talk? Some consultant she was if they wouldn't listen. Well, she had her own dreams of being flower girl to think of. However, she had not forgotten that Grandma had offered to do *her* a favor.

Before Margaret could ask for permission to go over to Michelle's to tell her about the wedding, the phone rang again. Tad beat Grandpa to the phone. "Hi, Daddy! Hi, Mommy!" he said. "Fine. Cars *zoom zoom.*" Then he stuck the receiver out and shouted, "Margaret! Phone!"

Margaret took the phone, and what she heard made it impossible for her to answer. Daddy was saying, "It's perfect! So perfect, and on sale to boot.

It's from a chain store. We picked it out here in San Francisco. They've called the order in to their store in Portland, and it will be delivered to your room today. I'd better talk to your grandpa, have him take your old bed into the other bedroom for Tad. Tad will think he's big, sleeping in your old bed."

Margaret, without saying a word back to the phone, simply handed the phone to Grandpa and said, "It's for you."

Grandpa acted very happy. He said, "Sure, sure. Of course I can. Of course I will. Store the crib on the rafters in the garage. Okay. Don't worry about Tad, we'll handle it. The space will be ready for the water bed by the time they get here."

So that's how it went. Adults were making decisions over her head. They were tearing her room apart. They even convinced Tad that this was the world's biggest event, having his crib torn down and her old bed sitting in the room next to Rusty's bed. The beds were twin beds, and it did look nice to have them together. But, even that hurt Margaret to see.

It was awful what adults can do to a kid's life. They never ever ask, they just *tell.* Margaret would have no part of it. She wished she could sleep in her old bed tonight. She had planned to let Tad have her old bed one day, but it was to have been replaced by a wonderful canopy bed. Margaret felt herself begin to cry.

Tad was hugging her, kissing her. "Margaret, Tad got big bed. I love 'oo, Margaret."

"I love you, too, Tad," Margaret sobbed.

Then Margaret left the house in order to be alone. She told Grandma that she was going to Michelle's, but actually she just wanted to be by herself. It was too late to use Mr. Simmons as her consultant. The damage was already done. She went slowly by the vacant lot, staring at the grass, the junk, just anything to keep from thinking or feeling. She spotted a bright piece of metal, sort of spoon-shaped. Tad would like that for playing in the sand. But she didn't stop. It'd mean getting down out of her wheelchair, and she didn't care enough to do that. It looked as if she'd never have a sports model, built low to the ground where it would be simple to reach out and pick things up.

When at last she felt like talking to Michelle, Michelle wasn't home. Margaret felt betrayed. Maybe if she just went around the block a couple of times and tried again, Michelle would be home.

She saw Mr. Simmons on his park bench. He'd be no help to her, but she might just go talk to him to make him smile and get that happy look into his old faded eyes. But first she had to smile, and right now she could not do it. She started to go on by, but he called, "Margaret? Margaret, is that you?"

Margaret turned and went slowly back towards him.

He said, "Where's your twin? You going to sing solo today?"

"I can't sing at all today. I'm getting a water bed."

"That's something to sing about. I got me one five years ago. I've slept pretty good since then. You'll be happy with it. Why the long face?"

"I . . . I . . . Mr. Simmons . . ."

His heavy veined hand touched her soft sweaty one, and so she told him everything. Just everything. And he didn't ask her to act dignified or responsible. In fact, she cried, and it seemed okay to do it.

At last, when her crying was over, he said to her, "Well, child, the world is not finished and done with because of one day. You've got lots more days in your life, and you'll find a way to do the things you want and have the things you want. Think how long you've got, Margaret. I'm ninety-three."

"And did you have a daughter who got to have a canopy bed?"

"No. No children. Of course, I had Robbie, and I have all you children. You know how people are telling you what you don't need? Well, every person I knew told me I didn't need to be buying a new house in a new subdivision just after my wife died. Well, what they didn't know was that she was my light and my joy, and I wasn't ready to give up either of those fine things. I had another joy in my work, you see. I was a geneticist. I worked breeding new plants. Time slowed me down a bit, but I needed to be in this new park with its new plants. The workmen often used me as a consultant."

"Is Robbie a gene-geneticist?" Margaret remembered that Robbie still used Mr. Simmons as a consultant.

"No, not quite." Mr. Simmons laughed. "No, he's more into investing, but I've done a bit of that myself, so we talk. I allow him to do what he likes, he approves of my having a house facing the park and doing what I like."

"Michelle doesn't like canopy beds," said Margaret.

"There, you see. But I bet she wouldn't mind if you owned one."

"Maybe not. She sure wants me to get my sports model."

"I want that for you, too, Margaret. And in all those days you've got ahead of you, I'll wager you'll find a way. You know what I'd like right now? A song. Do you think you feel up to it?" She tried, and she could, and she felt much better. She said goodbye then and went back to see Michelle.

But Michelle still wasn't home. It would feel too awkward to go back to Mr. Simmons again. She guessed she'd go see the Bernstein twins. At the last minute, she remembered it was their day for piano. But Rosalee and Rachel were still having their end-of-the-summer yard sale. Their mother was running it until they got home from piano lessons. Margaret figured she'd waste some time there, looking things over. Why not buy $33.30 worth of stuff? What good did it do her to save money when Daddy hadn't given her the chance to present her case. It really was a very sneaky thing he'd pulled, to have paid for the water bed already and have it on the way to their house before she was told. Maybe she'd just buy sixty-six of the Bernsteins' twin dresses.

Actually there were very few clothes at the yard sale. Mostly this was Mrs. Bernstein's stuff. There was a light with a very long gold chain on it. It was the kind of light that hangs high from the ceiling, and the very long chain drapes and reaches down to an outlet near the floor. The light globe was all cracked. Price: 25¢. If the globe hadn't been cracked, Margaret would gladly have paid the twenty-five cents. She liked the gold chain. There were some pretty gold ashtrays, but no one Margaret knew smoked. There were lots of chipped dishes. Margaret wondered if the twins also tried to balance things. Then Margaret spotted some beautiful cloth lying on top of some curved pieces of wood. It was white eyelet. Maybe a beautiful dress. Margaret examined the material. It wasn't a dress. What was it? It had some seams.

Mrs. Bernstein came over. "You interested in that canopy top, Margaret? My twins have decided not to be twins anymore. Rosalee is getting rid of her canopy top and her majorette costume and her Barbie collection and goodness knows what all. At least Rachel is keeping her head about her things. I told Rosalee she's not going to be able to redo her whole life with the proceeds of this rummage sale, but she won't listen. You want that? You can have it for three dollars."

A canopy top! Margaret's gloom lifted entirely. But first she had to ask Mrs. Bernstein to repeat the offer just to make sure this wasn't all her imagination. She did have a very good imagination. But Mrs. Bernstein said, "Oh, I'm afraid it's all too real. Well, you want it? Can someone help you get it home? I'm glad it's you that's getting it, Margaret."

"I'll take it," whispered Margaret. "I'll be back with the three dollars."

It seemed to take her hours to get home and get the money and also get Rusty to agree to help her carry the canopy back from Mrs. Bernstein's. Rusty kept saying, "Margaret, this is dumb. Water beds don't have big posts on them to hold up a canopy."

"I know that," said Margaret. Really she didn't know that. She had never seen a water bed, but Rusty had. His friend's parents had one. "I wanted a canopy, and I'm getting a canopy. Rusty, don't you see? It was meant for me to have it, or else Rosalee wouldn't have decided to sell hers right this minute."

"That's dumb, Margaret."

Dumb or not, Margaret paid her three dollars and had Rusty balance the folded wood pieces on the handles of her wheelchair. She held the pretty cloth in her lap, and they hurried home, stopping only once when Margaret asked Rusty to pick up the metal spoon-shaped object from the ground for Tad. Margaret stopped short when she saw, in front of their house on the curb, a large box and some packing lying around. So the water bed was already set up.

Rusty took the canopy stuff and, except for a slight pause to flip the metal spoon-shaped object on the hood of the Sprite, raced on inside.

Margaret wheeled in through the garage, up the wooden ramp Daddy had built for her, through the family room, and then down the hall to her bedroom. There it was. Grandma and Grandpa stood beside it, beaming. "Like it, Margaret?" Grandma asked.

"It's too big," said Margaret. Then, she didn't like the sad looks on her grandparents' faces, and she knew she should act responsible, at least. "I guess all water beds are big," she said.

"Only about eighteen inches wider than your old bed, Margaret. Here, let me plop you on it." Then Grandpa picked Margaret up as if she were helpless and plopped her onto her water bed.

"I could have gotten here myself, Grandpa." Her body was swaying a bit with the water. Then Tad jumped on, and Rusty jumped on, and they all had a good time rolling and tumbling over on the squishy bed. Mother would have died if she had known they were doing this.

Margaret was almost having fun when Grandpa asked, "What's this?"

Rusty answered, "It was Margaret's dumb idea. She got it at a yard sale for three dollars. I told her water beds don't have posts to hold up a canopy.

Anyway, Margaret, it's not wide enough for this bed."

Grandpa said, "Rusty, some water beds do have posts, but you were right that this one doesn't. Now, you don't talk for a minute, and let's hear why Margaret bought this."

"It was what I wanted," whispered Margaret, and it really hurt to admit she'd been so dumb.

"I . . . I . . ." she began.

"I'll haul the canopy back out to the garage," interrupted Rusty. "It can just lay around broken-down like Daddy's Sprite. I guess she's like Daddy. Just likes to own something even if it is broken-down." He picked up the folded mess.

"Just a minute," said Grandpa. "I wish there was some way we could make some posts to hold that canopy up there at the ceiling so Margaret could look up at it and enjoy it. Let's see."

Grandpa's wish gave magic to Margaret's mind. She shouted, "It can swing from the ceiling on a gold chain like the lamp does." She rolled herself to the edge of her water bed and was onto her wheelchair. "I'll be right back with the chain. I know just where it is, and I have the twenty-five cents."

So she bought the very long chain from Mrs. Bernstein, who let her have it for twenty cents since Margaret did not want the lamp part. Grandpa divided it into four equal pieces. He hooked the short chains to the ceiling and the lower end of each chain

to a corner of the canopy. Then up went the beautiful eyelet cover.

Margaret moved back to the doorway to size it all up. It was true the water bed was wider, sticking out a bit in front and beneath her window, but the window curtains and the jaunty flounce to the eyelet somehow gave it all artistic balance. "It's lovely," said Margaret. "Thank you, Grandpa, it's perfectly lovely."

It wasn't a sports-model wheelchair, but at least the canopy overhead kept her looking up.

Margaret Saves
the Wedding

Mother and Daddy were surprised and very pleased to see that Margaret's water bed had become a canopy bed as well. And Daddy spent at least two hours raving about Margaret and Rusty's summer job. It was great while it lasted! But long before Margaret was tired of the praise, Mother and Grandma began talking about the wedding. Mother was thrilled to think Tad would be the ring bearer.

Margaret wasn't sure. "Tad's only two, and he just loves to smash things down. It'll never work," she warned.

"But Margaret, there just aren't any other boys in the family that are the right age. All he has to do is walk. He'll do just fine because he'll be walking right in back of you and just before your cousins who will be bridesmaids."

It might work. Tad did like to run along in back of Margaret's wheelchair, but sometimes he'd hop on the back of it. She'd have to talk to him about proper actions, talk to him every day and every night, and then it still might not work.

It's just as well she had to spend so much time talking to Tad because she certainly couldn't talk to Rusty, who always was away for soccer practice, nor to Daddy. Daddy never liked to be talked to when he was working on his Sprite. He'd worked on it day and night ever since he had found the spoon-shaped lever to the fuel pump lying on the hood. Rusty never admitted he put it there. Margaret figured Rusty lost it the day he raced out of the garage to get the balloon from the mall, but she didn't tell. Anyway, Daddy had begun work on the Sprite even before Grandma and Grandpa left, mumbling something about having kept Mother waiting too long already.

Before Grandma left, she reminded Margaret of the favor she still owed her. Margaret couldn't think of anything at first. But finally she asked Grandma to call and find out the cost of a sports model. The answer was an astounding *thousand dollars.* A demonstration model had been made in a child's size, the salesman said. He would be happy to ship it to Portland so Margaret could try it out over a weekend.

Mother said, "Definitely not. Margaret's hopes are too high as it is."

So, Margaret had gone out to the garage and begged Daddy at least to make the trip to the showroom. He said, "All right, Margaret. Now run along. I think I've just about got this baby licked. Tell your mother I've got things moving at last!" His mind was on the Sprite, not the wheelchair.

Margaret figured he had agreed without even knowing it, but he was a great promise-keeper no matter how the promise was gotten from him. She reported to Mother what he had said and also that he'd promised to take her to the showroom.

Mother ignored the part about the showroom. She just said, "He's still a long way from selling that car. No car like the Sprite sells unless there's someone who wants to buy it, and that someone has to know who has it. Things don't always work out so easily."

Margaret went back to Daddy and suggested that maybe she and Rusty could have a real garage sale and sell his Sprite. He laughed and said, "Thanks, honey, but this is hardly a garage-sale item. No, I'll have to advertise in a couple of papers. Now, run along and let me finish this." So she ran along to the park and told Mr. Simmons everything—about the promised trip to the showroom and about Daddy's Sprite being almost ready to sell and all about the wedding.

Aunt Patty sent a picture and a pattern number

for the dress Margaret was to wear as flower girl. She also sent a check for twenty-five dollars for the material and had asked Mother to make it. Patty had chosen white and yellow daisies for her flowers, and Margaret was to carry a bouquet of them.

Mother said, "Why, that white dress you bought with the yellow embroidered daisies will be a perfect match. I'll call and tell her and send back her check."

Margaret spent the following days preaching to Tad about how to walk and letting him practice by carrying a sofa pillow down the hall behind her. A couple of times, he got silly and dropped the pillow or got tired and threw it down. So Margaret said to Mother, "You really must get someone else to be ring bearer before it's too late."

Mother held up a little yellow satin suit she had made the night before, after the rest of the family had all gone to bed. She said, "Sorry, it's already too late. Adorable, isn't it?"

It was a beautiful little suit with knicker pants. Rusty said, "Yeck! It looks like mustard has landed all over it. Tad, you'll have to dig the rings out of the mustard, and Scott will get mustard all over his hands when he tries to put it on Aunt Patty's finger, and he'll slip, and the mustard will fly in your face, Tad, and . . ."

"Stop that!" Mother shouted.

Rusty said, "I'm just talking to Tad, to get him ready for the wedding, just like Margaret does."

"I do not," Margaret shouted right back. "Rusty, you are sickening! You're positively sickening!"

"Ickening! Ickening!" sang Tad. "Rusty ickening!" he said it again and again. He even ran out to the Sprite and looked under the car at Daddy and shouted, "Daddy ickening!" It didn't stop there. He said it to just anybody and everybody he saw for the next few days. Margaret was scared to death that he might even say it to the wedding guests. He certainly said it to the salesman that Friday night when they went to look at the demonstration sports model.

The salesman didn't understand Tad or was not really listening to him. He was busy having a price discussion with Daddy. "No," the salesman told Daddy, "the chair cannot be purchased on time. We could give you the name of a bank that makes small loans."

Daddy explained that he already had some pretty large loans, but Daddy was watching Margaret as he spoke. Margaret wanted the whole entire world to watch her. She was zipping around the showroom in that lightweight chair, whirling around in a *very* small space and then speeding back to hear their words again. Rusty and Tad were chasing her.

"Do it again," shouted Rusty. "Do another wheelie, Margaret."

Then Margaret made the most wonderful discovery of all: By popping the front wheels up high, she could actually go up a step to a higher floor in the showroom. She raced back *very* fast to tell Daddy.

Daddy reached his hand out to stop her, but the salesman said, "It's all right. No danger if she speeds. She has a stop bar on front, and the wheels are set for it. It won't turn over. It's a very stable machine."

Margaret already knew that. She'd felt the wheels set on a slight angle, and she just knew it was safe to speed. Besides, she'd seen those men at the basketball game do it. She pulled another wheelie and went up the stair as the salesman said to Daddy, "No, we do not take used wheelchairs as a trade-in."

Tad shouted, "You ickening!" at the salesman and came running after Margaret.

Daddy said, "Well, thanks for showing us. One of these days when we get a thousand dollars together, we just may be back. I am impressed."

"You're welcome to take it home for the weekend," the salesman said.

"No," said Daddy, "that's not necessary."

"Oh, please, Daddy, it's the wedding weekend. Can't I use it just for the wedding?"

"Oh, why not?" said Daddy, and then everyone was happy. Margaret wheeled out to their car, and the salesman showed Daddy how to fold it.

Tad told the salesman once more, "You ickening!" and away they went home to show Mother.

The next day, Margaret went to the park to show it to Mr. Simmons and to see how smoothly it would go over the little curved bridge, but she was very careful to keep it clean for the wedding Sunday afternoon.

Michelle and Rosalee and Rachel came out to join in the fun. Of course, the most fun was Margaret's. She was always right along even with them when they walked about the park, and she could laugh at all the right words and not have to call for them to wait up and say things again.

"I think it is absolutely super," said Rosalee.

"I think it is super-duper," said Michelle.

"I'd like to give it a try just once, if you don't mind," said Rachel.

Margaret didn't mind. So they all had a try while Mr. Simmons watched. He said, "Well, Margaret, now you know exactly what you're aiming for. I'm glad you got to try it out this weekend."

"Me, too," said Margaret. "I better go home now so I keep it clean for the wedding. I'll come show you my bouquet, Mr. Simmons. Daisies. I'll even let you smell them." She laughed with him merrily and then went speeding away real fast for home.

The wedding day came up sunny, which was a miracle for Portland, Mother said. There was a little fancy-roofed pavilion that the bride and groom could have used in case of rain, but all the guests' chairs were outside. There really were lots of guests. Even Michelle said so. The Bernstein twins agreed. They had seen three weddings this summer, and they knew and were not just saying that to please

Margaret. They admired the yellow satin sash Mother had made to go on Margaret's dress. And they loved the wreath of daisies Margaret wore in her hair and the garland of them draped on the low back of her sports model. They all had to smell the bouquet. With all the fuss about the flowers, Tad begged to carry the bouquet. When she told him no, that he must carry the rings, he even called her ickening.

Michelle whispered, "Your sports model really has class. I *know* someday, you'll get to keep it."

Oh, it was great to have good friends! Margaret's friends were not truly invited guests, but had come as singers as they had done at the other weddings. Only this time, Margaret could not go the rounds with them before the wedding. She had to stay by Tad and see that he did not fall down and get his suit dirty.

She took Tad to say hello to Mr. Simmons, who would be watching this wedding, same as all the others. Besides, she had promised to let him smell her bouquet. He said, "Margaret, you and your little brother both look just perfect. I'm delighted you could be in your sports model for the wedding."

Margaret said, "I know. Oh, I wish it were really mine and not just a demonstrator! But I'm glad I have it for this weekend. One day, when we can afford it, when we get a thousand . . ." She stopped, for there was someone else listening. A man as old as Grandpa was sitting beside Mr. Simmons today.

Mr. Simmons introduced him at once. "Margaret, I'd like you to meet Robbie."

It took a lot of control for Margaret to say in return, "I'm pleased to meet you, Robbie." She had never called a man as old as Grandpa by his first name. And, besides, she'd always imagined the Robbie Mr. Simmons spoke of as being quite young. She had forgotten just how very old Mr. Simmons was, she guessed. Anyway, Robbie was a very pleasant, well-dressed man. Soon she forgot about his age or his name being different, and she had Mr. Simmons hold her bouquet while she showed Robbie how fast she could go in her sports model and how she could pull a wheelie to turn fast or to climb up on the sidewalk.

Tad ran after her so fast that he fell. Robbie picked Tad up and dusted him off. Tad shouted, "You ickening!" and ran to Margaret to be loved.

"What was that he said?" Robbie asked.

"I don't think you want to know," answered Margaret. "I think I better get him back over to the bridge before the wedding starts without us."

"Not so fast, Miss Margaret. Mr. Simmons tells me your father's interested in sports cars. I'm a little bit partial to certain sports models myself. I came today hoping to meet your father."

Old Mr. Simmons was chuckling. "Saying he's interested in sports cars is like saying he's interested in breathing. He's always been interested in sports cars. His dad used to tell him it was a hobby he couldn't afford, but he'd go buy one all torn up and fix it just as your daddy does, Margaret. Now he no longer does the fixing, but he's interested in other people who do. No one can say he can't afford anything these days. I hope you don't mind that I brought him here today to meet your father. You want to tell him the *kind* of car your father's interested in selling? Now Robbie, I didn't know this myself until just last week when Margaret told me."

"It's a 1962 Austin Healey Sprite," answered Margaret, being very aware that she might be matching Daddy up with a buyer. "It's shiny dark green. It's a very nice car. Daddy says it's really great to ride in it with the top down and let the wind blow your hair." Margaret had ridden in a convertible once, and she wasn't quite sure she liked all that much wind in her hair, but she realized other people did.

"Where does he keep this Sprite? Does he have a buyer yet?" Robbie looked eager.

"He keeps it in our garage. But pretty soon he'll put an ad in the paper. That's how to sell a car."

Robbie jumped up from the bench, practically knocking Tad over again. Tad began to yell anew, "Ickening, ickening, ickening!" until Margaret could hardly hear Robbie say, "Do you think it's possible to see your father before the wedding?"

Mr. Simmons said, "Now Robbie, there's no need to rush, we have . . ."

"Tad, be quiet," Margaret said. "We've got to go get Daddy really quick."

It wasn't all that hard to find Daddy, because he

was coming to find them and was scolding, "Margaret, this is your aunt's wedding. Let's not ruin it by being late." He scooped up Tad and was pushing against Margaret's shoulders, making her sports model move even faster than she could make it go.

But Margaret grabbed his arm. "I think a man wants to buy your Sprite," she said, and that stopped Daddy cold. Then the wedding music began, and he moved fast again. Quickly, loudly, she told him what Mr. Simmons' friend Robbie had said. Daddy handed Tad over to Mother and gave Margaret a push to her place in the lineup.

He whispered something to Mother that ended with, "Look, I'm tempted to go back there and see that man before he leaves and I miss this big chance. It'd only take a couple of minutes. I'm just the usher, and that's all done by now."

Mother said, "Patty will never forgive you, nor will I."

"Just kidding. I wouldn't leave, of course. You know, I bet I could get enough from a collector to buy you a small van. Gas mileage wouldn't matter for just around town, and we could use it to take the kids camping. Why, I bet I could get enough to even give Margaret a finder's fee, set the money aside for her towards that wheelchair. That would be great for her. I just hadn't realized how much more freedom that chair offers her. Gee, I hope that guy sticks around until this wedding's over." Daddy was so nervous, but his face was wreathed in smiles. He was fairly dancing with excitement.

Tad said, "Daddy ickening."

Margaret's stomach was all aflutter from what she'd just heard Daddy say. There was certainly her own money to help the fund grow, and she could earn more, lots more. The wedding march began. That was Margaret's cue. Her stomach became a real fluttery mess now, but her hands spun the wheels of the sports-model wheelchair. One day it would be her very own—she was sure of it.

Now she was out and away, the first to move forward to go up and over the curved bridge to the minister who waited on the other side to read the wedding vows. The audience was all seated to the right of her and was watching, of course. It made her quite nervous. Rusty was in the front row, all dressed up in his Sunday suit and smiling a missing-tooth smile. He was being a good sport about missing his big soccer game. Margaret hoped Tad was following behind her. He must have been, because the crowd began to laugh, and he began to yell at them, "You ickening!"

"Quiet, Tad, quiet!" Margaret said without moving her head back. A wedding was supposed to be very proper and dignified. Tad did get quiet when the audience stopped laughing, and Margaret rolled up and over the little bridge. She looked back ever so slightly to see if Tad was following, and she got a quick glimpse of shining yellow and knew that he was. At last they came to the spot where Tad was to stand beside her and wait for the bridesmaids and then the bride. He stood, and Margaret relaxed.

Well, little two-year-old Tad had done just fine. Mother was right, after all.

Ah, there was Patty. What a beautiful bride! Her dress flowed over the entire path, and when she moved up over the bridge, she was like a soft white cloud moving through the beautiful Japanese garden. Margaret would like her own wedding to be like this. Hey, Tad was moving also!

"Oh, no!" said Margaret.

"Ball!" Tad shouted as he ran away to the left side of the grounds where a vine-covered fence separated the soccer field from the Japanese garden. A soccer ball had made it over the fence. Quickly, Margaret stuck the stem of her bouquet under her yellow satin sash so both hands were free. Then, a fast wheelie and she was off after Tad.

Without those rings, the wedding would be stopped before it was begun. Tad was almost as fast a runner as Rusty. Still she must catch him. She sped along like the wind, but it was not fast enough. Then there was a flash of red hair, and Rusty ran past her and had the cushion swept out of Tad's hands and was on his way back to the bride and groom before Margaret could reach Tad—even in her sports model.

Margaret felt sick inside, knowing now for certain that she'd never be as fast as her brothers, but she pushed back that feeling and gave her full attention to Tad. Rusty had done some quick running to save the rings. Now she must do some quick thinking to

save Tad from ruining the wedding. He had forgotten about the soccer ball already and was stamping his foot and screaming, "My rings! Rusty got my rings!"

"Tad, oh please, Taddy, don't scream. Here, here, you can hold my flowers."

"Rings! Tad's rings!" At least he was not screaming so loudly.

Quick—she must think of something else to say to him. Weddings are supposed to be very dignified. She took the garland that was draped on the back of her wheelchair and draped it around Tad's neck. "There, there're *your* flowers, Tad. Say, Taddy-boy, *you* look great!"

Tad's eyes grew bright, and he stopped pouting. He grinned instead. "Tad's great!" he proclaimed.

"Right," said Margaret and straightened her skirt and brushed back her hair. "Now follow me just like we've practiced. Good boy, Tad." Her left hand held up her bouquet of daisies properly now, and her right hand pushed against the wheel, and then serenely she began her journey back to take part in the wedding.

Rusty, who had said he'd not be a part of the wedding group, was now very much a part of it. Also, from the corner of her eye, Margaret saw a group of uninvited guests standing up in back of the seated guests. It was Rusty's soccer team! Every last boy and girl on the team was standing there witnessing eight-year-old Rusty be ring bearer. She guessed they were waiting until after the wedding so they could go across the grounds to get their ball—there was no other way across, except where the wedding was taking place. Rusty didn't flinch, but rather proudly held up the cushion while waiting for Margaret and Tad to take their places.

To one side of the soccer team stood Margaret's friends, the other members of the sextet, next to Mr. Simmons and Robbie, who were seated on the park bench. The girls were waving to her, and she wanted to wave back, but instead she smiled, just a little in a dignified wedding style, and they waved even more.

Everyone was quiet and still, even Tad, while the wedding vows were said. Scott became Uncle Scott. He took the ring from the cushion that Rusty held and put it on Aunt Patty's finger. She put the other ring on Scott's finger. Margaret was indeed proud of Rusty for having saved the rings so the wedding could take place. And she was quite proud of herself when Mother said it was truly Margaret who had saved the wedding itself, that things couldn't have gone more smoothly and the wedding had been just perfect!

And it was all right that Daddy wasn't there to join in the praise. He was quickly moving in the direction of Robbie and Mr. Simmons. From all their smiles, Margaret felt sure that her finder's fee would bring the total on her wheelchair fund way up. She'd have enough in no time at all! She was on her way.